I0417803

the DAGGER

A NOVEL BY

TIMOTHY GEORGE

This is a work of fiction. This is a novel, and to construe it as anything else would be an error. Names, characters, places, and incidents are either the product of the author's imagination or are used fictitiously. Any resemblance to actual persons, living or dead, real events, or locales is entirely coincidental.

Copyright © 2016 Timothy George
MVP Publishing Group LLC
www.mvppublishinggroup.com

All rights reserved. Printed in the United States of America. No part of this book may be used or reproduced in any manner whatsoever without written permission of the publisher, except in the case of brief quotations embodied in critical articles and reviews.

Library of Congress Control Number: 2016908766
ISBN-13: 978-0-9852364-2-7 (paperback)
ISBN-13: 978-0-9852364-3-4 (ebook)

Interior & Cover Design: Dana Pittman

For David Nathaniel (1955 – 2014).

ACKNOWLEDGMENTS

I am extremely grateful to those whose contributions have enhanced this work. I want to thank my family and friends for their support and encouragement to make this book a reality.

CHAPTER 1

The window shade let a glint of sunlight into a small room with dull blue walls that was filled with the aroma of antiseptic chemicals. The fine sliver of light found its mark on the bed where Thomas Jet, the Chicago investment banker, lay semiconscious. Thoughts rambled about in his head: images of Chicago, his father, and Uncle Jessie, along with bits and pieces of memories he thought were only bizarre dreams. When the cloud moved away from covering the sun again, the light was directly in his left eye. The brightness caused Thomas to wake up to discover his other eye and the rest of his face were covered with bandages and gauze. Thomas attempted to raise his hands, but his body was restrained to the bed. He could see that his fingertips were covered in bandages as well. He thought, *Am I disfigured?* Mr. Jet then lost consciousness falling back into a deep sleep.

Weeks later, a frail man in a white coat entered the dimly lit room. The squeak from rusted hinges on the metal door alerted Thomas of the man's presence. He raised his head. The man said, "You're awake, finally. I was getting worried about you. You are almost healed. In just twenty-four hours, I will take off the bandages. We had to restrain you to prevent injury to your new face while you slept." The thin man chuckled gently, lifting the gauze around Thomas's nose, chin, and mouth to examine him.

Thomas mumbled, "What…happened?" Thinking he had been in a coma after a terrible accident, Thomas strained to see anything familiar, but the cramped little room offered no comfort. There were no cards or flowers from friends wishing him a speedy recovery. Thomas felt the emptiness of being alone. His mind was full of questions, and he was fearing the worst: that his face was disfigured.

"Don't speak," said the doctor, touching his finger to Thomas's lips. "You have stitches in your mouth too. I will take them out tomorrow. You will be a new person, just wait." The pale thin man smiled proudly as if he were happy with his work. The doctor whispered, "The drugs accelerated your healing and made you sleep. The side effect is your memory loss, but everything will come back to you eventually. Sleep now." The doctor closed the blinds securely, and the light was gone.

Hours later, in the darkness, a shadowy figure appeared in the corner across the room. Thomas strained to see, but his eyes were too weak to make out the shape. Then there was a whisper, "Don't break the chain." Thomas remembered the voice. It was Maalik, the former director of intelligence of the Brotherhood, the African secret society that had come into existence a millennium ago.

Maalik…he's dead, Thomas thought. His body had been discovered in Paris four months earlier.

The raspy voice continued, "There's much to do and not much time. Sinister forces are gathering in Spain, looking toward Africa. Wake up! It's in your hands now." The ghostly figure then vanished into dust. Startled by the eerie vision, Thomas shook his head then went back to sleep, thinking the dream was just another side effect from the medication that made him sleep.

The next day, slowly, the forgotten memories trickled in one by one. He remembered the mysterious Dr. Oble, with his hat and bow tie, the one who had enticed Thomas to seek his real father and his link to the African Brotherhood. The voice of Miss Erd, a psychic master and his lover, penetrated the drug's side effects, which clouded Thomas's mind. Thomas felt her presence. His own psychic powers were reviving. He remembered his induction ceremony when he joined the Brotherhood at Rock Creek Park. The pain flashed to Thomas's mind, reminding him of the time when he cut his finger to take the oath of secrecy. His mind sparked with vivid flashbacks of the underwater cave in Belize and the life he left behind in Chicago; he was saddened to think that he would never return to his comfortable life. He now understood why he felt so lonely.

An accident did not put Thomas Jet in bed, wrapped like a mummy. The faint distant sounds of bells were familiar to him. *Paris*, he thought. The sound of bells from Notre Dame lingered in his mind. Now he remembered arranging for the plastic surgery procedure to change his face and remove his fingerprints to make his final transformation as the new leader of the Brotherhood's intelligence section. Three weeks ago, Thomas oversaw the dismantling of the underground intelligence compound in Cape Verde and scattered the intelligence branch into smaller groups throughout Africa and Europe.

The Brotherhood's legacy spanned almost a thousand years. It was founded by representatives from seven ancient African kingdoms. The mission of the group, as Dr. Oble, his first contact, explained it, was to preserve African history and prepare for the rebirth of the continent. Dr. Oble traveled the world, selecting individuals such as Thomas to become the future leaders of the organization. Thomas, like all the others before him, was connected to the founders of the Brotherhood through the blood of his family line.

Before departing for Paris for his surgery, Thomas inspected his new command center on a converted Turkish two-hundred-foot fishing trawler equipped with a helipad and a crew of twenty-four. The idea of using a ship for his headquarters came from his adventure in the Gulf of Mexico while in search of treasure. The overhauled ship was designed to maintain the appearance of a trawler for stealth reasons, but it had been retrofitted with enhanced engines, state of the art technology, and defensive weapons systems. Thomas loved the sea from his days in Chicago, but most importantly, he valued the flexibility to move his intelligence headquarters to any location in the world. The new ship was named *Scorpion*.

The next day, the doctor removed the wrapping from Thomas's face and handed him a mirror. Thomas looked at his reflection and saw a stranger.

CHAPTER 2

An unexpected winter snowstorm quickly covered the ground with several feet of fresh white powder. Traffic ground to a halt. Newark Liberty International Airport, as well as JFK and the remaining airports on the Eastern Seaboard, closed for the winter storm. Simon had not slept well during the sixty days since the shipment of diamonds arrived at his office. He reflected on his days in corporate America, now he was surrounded by a mountain of rare diamonds. Security was tightened, but the vast fortune of diamonds could tempt anyone. No one knew where the diamonds were stored, except his colleagues in the Brotherhood: Brother Dawson, Goode, and Pete.

Simon arranged to sell at auction a small lot of diamonds through a diamond broker located in Amsterdam. Actually, the Bittle law firm in DC made the arrangements for the sale through a series of dummy corporations set up in the Cayman Islands. The transaction netted more than Simon had expected. The size of the stones created a buzz in the diamond industry. The final bid was four hundred and fifty million dollars. When Simon got the call from his lawyer, he was surprised. *This was a little more than ten percent of our inventory*, he thought.

His joy soon turned to worry. News eventually would spread about the unusually large diamonds. People would start asking questions and speculating on the source. The syndicate of diamond men would start losing market share and seeking out their competition. Even though they had been very careful, using layers of secrecy about who actually controlled the diamonds, it was no longer safe to keep the diamonds in New Jersey. The diamonds had to be moved out of the warehouse to a more secure location. Simon and Pete sorted the more valuable, large, blue diamonds and packaged them into smaller lots for shipment to two banks with special vaults located in Switzerland. The other stones were also impressive, but not like the blue diamonds. The remainder was destined for vaults in the top-tier banks in Switzerland. Simon trusted no one but the Brotherhood to handle the stones. This meant that only Simon and his newfound Brotherhood could do the tedious work of preparing the precious stones for shipment.

Goode and Dawson traveled to Europe with the last shipment of blue diamonds. The two men arrived at the Citizen de Rouge Bank located on a quiet street near Kochergasse in Bern, Switzerland.

"This is the last stop. After we deposit these packages, we are done," said Goode, crossing off nine other banks from his list. The bank officer escorted the two men into the vault. He departed to allow the men privacy to lock away the precious stones. Each bank had special instructions to change the account numbers and safe access authority twenty-four hours after each deposit. The new accounts and security codes were sent to an undisclosed location where even Simon had no access. Only the elders of the Brotherhood were privy to this information. Before Maalik died, he outlined how the diamonds should be secured. Maalik understood the temptation would be too great to leave this information with anyone but the elders. He also knew if any of the brothers were captured and tortured, the secret would eventually be retrieved before death.

"I think we need to count the stones in this package. Do you have the list and package count?" Goode pulled out his knife to open the package. He continued, "This one feels light for some reason."

"Yeah, I have the list. Package 20114, blue diamonds, it should contain twenty-two stones," Dawson read from a computer printout.

Goode counted out the stones and then counted again. He said, "Something is not right. The count is off. You count."

Dawson counted, "Eighteen, nineteen, twenty—that's it, twenty stones. There are two diamonds missing."

"Who signed the log for this package?" asked Goode.

"Pete, I think. It's scribbled, but it looks like Pete's writing."

Pete Joseph was one of the seven men located by Dr. Oble in America. He was identified as a descendant of one of the founders of the African Brotherhood. Dr. Oble found Pete at a casino in Atlantic City. He was once a schoolteacher, but discovered blackjack ten years ago. He called himself a professional gambler when Dr. Oble met him. His life changed when he agreed to join the Brotherhood.

"You don't think Pete would steal from the Brotherhood," whispered Dawson.

"Those diamonds could be worth several million dollars. He claims he gave up gambling, but who knows," whispered Goode.

"What do we do? We can't accuse him without proof."

"Let's finish up here," said Goode as he closed the package and placed the last of the diamonds in the vault.

* * * * *

Back in New Jersey, Simon paced the floor, waiting for a call from Goode to confirm that the last of the diamonds had been safely deposited in the vault in Switzerland. Pete was asleep on the sofa, having drunk too much the night before. He was snoring loud enough to rattle the glass on the coffee table.

The phone rang. Simon answered, and a voice asked, "Simon, you alone?"

"No, Pete's here. Don't you hear him snoring?"

"Go to another room, I need to talk to you," responded Goode.

"Okay, I am in the hall. Did you finish?"

"Yes, it's done. The funds from the auction arrived this morning. Four hundred fifty million dollars for the smaller lot of diamonds is better than I expected," whispered Goode with a smile. Then he got serious. "We have a problem. Two large blue stones are missing. We counted twice. Package 20114 only contained twenty stones."

Simon pulled out his PDA to check the list and said, "There should be twenty-two stones in that package. Pete sorted most of the blue stones."

"Yeah, he scribbled his signature like he didn't want it to be readable."

"What should we do?" asked Simon, thinking about the Brotherhood's rules for stealing and profiteering.

"You know what to do. Confront Pete and give him twenty-four hours to return the diamonds. If the stones are not returned, the Obsidians will deal with him," Goode said, his tone angry.

"They will kill him," said Simon.

"He may be already dead. Get the diamonds back. It's not our call," said Goode as he terminated the call.

Goode departed Switzerland for Ghana. Dawson returned to New Jersey.

* * * * *

Simon returned to the conference room and slammed the door, waking up Pete. Pete jumped. "Is it done? I am exhausted. We worked seventy-two hours sorting those diamonds. We've been locked up here for a week. I need to go home."

"Yes, they finished the delivery, and we are done, except for one thing."

"What's that?"

"We are missing two blue diamonds. They are worth a lot of money," said Simon, pacing the floor and looking at his watch.

"Two stones. Let's go look in the warehouse," responded Pete.

"You go ahead. I need to call the Obsidians. You know we have to report this kind of thing."

"Don't call those murderers. Why call them? Let's go look for the diamonds. They may have fallen out of the package." Pete was starting to perspire as he raised his voice.

"Calm down, Pete, this is the procedure. If I don't call them, they will come for me. We all swore a blood oath to the Brotherhood. The Obsidians watch over us. They may be listening now. You go ahead and look." Simon sent a text message to the elder who was in charge of the Obsidian Order in the United States and then put away his phone.

Pete left the room and then came back. He said, "Suppose I know where the stones are?"

"Did they fall out on the warehouse floor?" shouted Simon, swinging his fist at Pete, hitting the wall instead.

"No, no…I took them." Pete trembled as he looked at the hole in the wall made by Simon's fist.

"Where are they? I cannot make any promises concerning your safety; you know the rules. I may not wait for the Obsidians. Maalik was clear when we accepted our place in the Brotherhood." Simon looked at Pete with disgust in his eyes. He kicked the trashcan across the room and papers scattered on the floor. Simon then called the elder to update the Obsidian leader on the status of the missing diamonds.

"I owed my bookie money. He threatened my family. Come on, Simon, it's me, Pete. I have a wife and kids," pleaded Pete, holding his wallet in his hands to show Simon pictures of his two children.

"Those diamonds do not belong to us. You have twenty-four hours to return them. That's all I can do," shouted Simon, shaking his fist at Pete's face. It disgusted him that his brother would lie and steal from the Brotherhood. "We all have families. We tell no one our secrets. You compromised our mission. If those diamonds got in the wrong hands, they would lead straight to us. What were you thinking? You should have come to me if you needed money," responded Simon, pushing Pete against the wall.

"Will you call them off?" pleaded Pete.

"The Obsidians are everywhere. I cannot stop them. They may have mercy if you return the stones. They report to the elders. Don't worry about your family. We take care of our own." Simon put on his coat and hat and walked out the door. He yelled back, "Lock the door when you leave."

Pete sat in the empty building thinking about his fate. He reached in his pocket and removed two blue diamonds. They sparkled in the light. For a moment he was hypnotized by the sight. Reluctantly, he placed the diamonds in Simon's desk drawer and locked the warehouse door behind him. Pete called his wife and spoke to his children, thinking he would never see them again. His mind wandered as he drove out of the parking lot and looked into the rearview mirror while thinking of the Obsidians. He muttered, "Damn assassins. Where are they? When will they come for me?"

* * * * *

The next day, Pete sat at a table in a cafeteria preparing to eat his last meal, or so he thought. A man approached him wearing a dark suit, black shirt, and no tie. He sat across the table from Pete and said, with a Jamaican accent, "Sir, do not let me disturb your meal."

"I've been expecting you. In fact, I was thinking this would be my last meal. Do we need to leave now?" Pete asked, with sweat starting to roll down his face.

"No, sir, enjoy your meal. You have plenty of time."

"Do you have some poison or something to make this quick?"

The man started laughing and then got serious. "Do not believe everything you hear about us. We have been watching you for months. We know all about your gambling debts and the threats to your family. Our surveillance equipment in the warehouse captured video of you taking the diamonds. We have surveillance cameras in Simon's office too."

"Why didn't you stop me?"

"That's not how we work. We saw that you turned over the diamonds when Simon challenged you."

"Yes, but if they had not found out, then I would have gotten away."

"Well, not really. We were waiting outside for you if you had not placed the diamonds in Simon's desk. Then things would have been unpleasant. We are watching everyone to see how they handle our business. Simon did the right thing. He followed the rules. Had he not done so, he would be sitting here with us. However, since you did the right thing, you got to enjoy this meal."

"But, but...What's next?"

"We paid your gambling debt this morning. Your bookie was warned to stay away from you. We broke his arm...by accident, but he is okay. Your family is safe."

"Thank you, thank you, brother—"

"Not so fast. Now you owe us what you owed the bookie."

"What? I thought—"

"No, the debt is still there. We figure you can work it off in two years."

"Two years doing what?"

"You volunteered to become an agent in the Obsidian Order. After your two years are up, you can rejoin the Brotherhood."

"What?"

"Yes, now finish your meal. Your training starts today."

Pete was relieved that his family was safe. As he ate his meal, he looked across the table at the massive man sitting before him, and he knew his life would never be the same again.

CHAPTER 3

Traveling the back roads to his lab, Brother Dawson enjoyed seeing the rolling hills of New Jersey. It reminded him of growing up in Kentucky, in bluegrass country. His father had worked as a trainer for a horse farm outside of Lexington. Even though Dawson acquired a love of riding horses, he spent most of his youth working on computers and studying puzzle books. As a child, he marveled at the challenge of solving mysteries. His classmates considered him a nerd. In college, he discovered a talent for swimming. He later joined the swim team. His skinny childhood body had now developed into a six-foot-two-inch frame with bulging biceps. Dawson discovered that being a swim-jock nerd was not all bad. He graduated with honors and earned his graduate degree on a swimming scholarship.

Though Brother Dawson had hoped one day to own a horse farm, those thoughts were now long gone. Never in Dawson's wildest dreams did he think he would graduate from MIT. However, becoming part of the Brotherhood was one of life's curveballs. Dawson had many doubts about the mystical side of the group, but he could not deny his connection to men such as Dr. Oble, Thomas, Goode, Simon, Jamal, and Pete. Being a man of science quickly made Dawson the go-to guy for unusual problems faced by his newfound band of brothers.

Six weeks earlier, in the early morning hours, Dawson met Miss Erd on her private plane at the Newark International Airport in New Jersey. Snow was still on the ground. Although Miss Erd had special psychic abilities, she brought with her an expert on ancient artifacts who specialized in medieval weapons. Erd had spent hours on the flight talking with a rotund, bearded art collector who devoted his life to studying weapons from the Middle Ages. They had passed the time talking about a mysterious object. He was a world-renowned expert on daggers of that period. The art collector had lost his eye as a child, and now he wore a black eye patch like a badge of honor. Miss Erd wanted Brother Dawson to hear, firsthand, the impressions that the expert had concerning the dagger.

Dawson boarded the plane in the hanger while Erd remained resting in the sleeping compartment. He introduced himself to the one-eyed man. Immediately, the strange-looking, pudgy fellow started talking about the mysterious dagger. "I have collected daggers for over fifty years, and this is the most unusual one I have ever encountered. It is an ornamental Moorish dagger. The blade is oversized with intricate grooves to the tip, an effective killing tool for close combat." The one-eyed man handed Dawson several large photographs of the dagger.

"Why do you say that?" asked Dawson.

With a coy look in his eye, the man whispered as he pointed at the photo of the dagger, "You see, it's easy to hide, but large enough to make deadly thrusts into vital organs like the lungs or heart. You know, Julius Caesar, the emperor of Rome, was killed with a dagger." The expert motioned with a wooden, twelve-inch ruler to demonstrate how to use the weapon. Breathing heavily, he thrust the ruler in a downward motion. "Even today, assassins favor this weapon." The expert smiled devilishly as he put the ruler back in his jacket pocket.

Dawson nodded but did not respond. He was thinking about the Obsidian Order, the Brotherhood's enforcers. They were skilled assassins known for their use of daggers.

After the demonstration, the one-eyed artifacts expert picked up the photo of the dagger and continued, "The dagger's blade is overlaid with a gold pattern. The handle is ivory, with unusual gemstones, which appear out of place for the period. For example, see the large emeralds, rubies, and quartz? And notice that the quartz stones are out of place. Why quartz and not diamonds? It is a remarkable specimen, priceless, but something is not quite right about it."

Erd entered the lounge and interrupted the men, saying, "Dawson, great to see you again. Have you seen the dagger?"

"Yes, but only in photos, though. I have taken plenty of notes from your expert," he said with a smile, pen in hand.

Dawson had not seen Erd since the time they spent together on the Cuban fishing boat in the Gulf of Mexico. He could not help but notice the radiant glow of her face and her smooth brown complexion. Her hazel eyes smiled at him. He had to look away for fear she could see his desire for her in his eyes. Dawson knew Erd was with Thomas, but seeing her in the silk, mauve-colored gown with a plunging neckline made him forget about Thomas. All he could think of at that moment was being with the strikingly beautiful black woman with perfect, kissable lips.

The gown fit her well. Her breasts were hidden, but the material gave way to the imprint of her nipples, and her finely sculpted body complemented the tight-fitting silk.

Erd opened the safe behind the bar and presented Dawson with a case with locks on the side. She opened the case to reveal the dagger. Erd noticed Dawson staring at her and said, "Brother Dawson, is something wrong?"

Startled, Dawson responded, "No, no. I am sorry. I haven't seen you in a while. Please forgive me for staring. Let us get to the business at hand."

Erd winked at Dawson. "Yes, let's do that. Thomas is counting on you. Remember?"

"Yes, Erd, I know. I'm ready for the challenge," said Dawson, embarrassed that Erd had caught him staring. He knew she had probably read his thoughts, too.

Dawson's eyes became fixed on the object. The connection was instantaneous, as had happened with Erd months earlier.

The one-eyed expert started talking again. "See the glow from the quartz stone…that's not right. They look radiant, like diamonds, but the stones are only quartz. Why?"

Erd cut him off, then handed Dawson the case.

"Who were the Moors?" said Dawson while holding the dagger.

"They were black or brown in complexion, and some were as dark as you," said Erd.

Dawson said, "They sound like Africans."

"Well, technically they are from North Africa. So yes, you could say that was true. This dagger was made somewhere in Moorish Spain. Our expert thinks it was made in Toledo more than one thousand years ago," said Erd as she put the dagger back in the case.

"Fascinating. How did the dagger end up in Zimbabwe?" asked Dawson.

"Good question, I don't know. Protect this with your life. Find the secret," whispered Erd as she made eye contact with Dawson while handing him the black leather-bound case.

The flight attendant escorted the one-eyed expert back to his seat as the pilot was making preparations to take off.

Dawson was left speechless by everything he had just heard. Miss Erd patted Dawson's hand as she walked him to the door and said, "Thomas has confidence that you will find the secret contained in this dagger. The Brotherhood is depending on you. All of our resources are at your disposal. God be with you my brother."

Dawson hugged Miss Erd and said confidently, "If there is something here, I will find it." He descended the stairs from the plane and then carefully placed the dagger case in the passenger seat of his car as he drove away from the airport.

* * * * *

Dawson's new laboratory was a converted dairy farm located in Vernon, New Jersey. The construction work was completed two months ago after he got word of the special project. Costs for the lab exceeded the budget of four million dollars. The new facility had reinforced walls and generators that allowed operations off the grid. All utility connections were severed except for a natural gas line contracted by a third party to power the generators. The lab had no wired connection to the outside world and had heavy security. Dawson relied on a satellite phone for communications with the Brotherhood.

The initial analysis of the dagger revealed what Erd and her expert had discovered. The scroll found inside the handle was translated with instructions to, "Follow the green light." He removed all the gemstones to examine the frame of the dagger. He found nothing out of the ordinary. The weight of the knife was consistent with its dimensions and the materials used. As a scientist, Dawson did not believe the dagger had any magical properties, and nothing dispelled this belief until he focused a laser on the emerald stones.

The laser produced images that projected writings in Sanskrit and diagrams on the wall that appeared to be design sketches for a device. Both emerald stones contained engraved information. Dawson took another look at the scroll found in the handle and discovered more writing previously hidden from view. The writings were in invisible oil and were only readable under a blue light. With that discovery, the hair on the back of Dawson's neck stood up.

Impossible, he thought, *such detail found encrypted in gemstones*. He carbon-dated some of the materials found on the dagger's sheath. The time period ranged in age from eight hundred to one thousand years for the leather pouch and the papyrus, which contained the writings. This was no magic. However, the technology to do this did not exist one thousand years ago, or so he thought. The information shown through the emerald's projections contained a series of complex formulas that resembled current-day physics. The formula was for an energy source for a device shown in the accompanying sketches. Materials for the device's components were described as silver, gold, lithium, and silicon dioxide (quartz) based on the translation of the ancient text.

Dawson's heart skipped a beat when he read the instructions of how to build a mysterious machine. He had no idea of its purpose. He called Thomas. "This is impossible. I don't know what the machine will do, even if we could build it. This could be dangerous."

"Can you build it? We must follow the prophecy. This is the key to our mission," prodded Thomas.

"It's possible, but I will need help. This formula for the power cell is a hybrid of a physics theory I've seen before. I will need to get my old professor involved to review the theory to determine if this actually would work. If I show him the text, he will recognize it, as I did," responded Dawson.

"Do you think he will keep our secrets?" queried Thomas.

"No, a scientific breakthrough like this could make him a Nobel Prize candidate. No amount of money will buy his silence. We would need to make arrangements before I approach him. We will also need to erase his memory through hypnosis," said Dawson.

* * * * *

The sports bar was overflowing with Red Sox fans who could not get tickets to the game with the Yankees. The smell of beer and the peanut shells that were scattered on the floor added to a familiar scene in the neighborhood pub that was frequented by college students. Dawson found himself reminiscing about his days at MIT. After a week of classes and labs, he would escape to the pub to drink beer, crack nuts, and catch up on sports. He did that many times. For a brief stint, he worked the bar when money fell short with his student loans. The owner treated Dawson like family during those lean years. His visit that day was not for the game.

Dawson had set up a meeting with his old physics professor, Dr. Easton. It was the only place the professor would agree to meet with students after classes. Dawson found a corner table in the back with a good view of the game to satisfy Dr. Easton's desire to see the end of the game. After his first beer, Dawson relaxed for a minute then drifted into deep thought, staring at the television monitor while his mind was back in his lab.

"Who's winning?" shouted Dr. Easton. "Do you need another beer?"

Startled, Dawson raised his mug to show his was half-full. He responded, "No, but bring some more nuts from the bar."

Dr. Easton arrived with more peanuts and his beer, holding a bundle of folders from class under his arm. He said, "What was the urgency? I thought you were chasing black gold in the oil fields. When did you get back in town?"

"I came in this afternoon on the train. I decided to take a break from the petroleum business. I've been looking at some of the theories from my last class with you and wanted to pick your brain," responded Dawson.

"Be careful, there is not much left up there," chuckled Dr. Easton. "What's this? You're thinking about physics again, after all these years? I had hoped you would finish your PhD, but the dollars from the oil industry were too strong to ignore. I don't blame you. Your career options would have been limited to research and teaching."

"I wish I had stayed with your program, but here I am today," said Dawson as he pulled out a yellow sheet of paper with a scrawl of notes and formulas. He handed the paper to Dr. Easton and then looked over to the TV to catch the rest of the game.

Moments passed as Dr. Easton casually glanced at the paper while pulling the shells from the peanuts and tossing the nuts in his mouth. He said, "Is this your work?"

"Not exactly. I am researching some writings from another scholar and found this to be interesting." Dawson looked back at the TV and sipped his beer, waiting for Easton's reaction to the information contained on the paper.

Dr. Easton pulled out his pen and started scribbling on the back of one of the folders he brought with him. He stopped drinking and eating and then mumbled, "This is impossible. Whose work is this? How did they figure this out? I've been working on this theory for twenty years and never got this close. What is this?"

Dawson said, "Is this possible? I thought of you when I finally understood the translation of the formula."

Easton responded, "Is there more? There are some missing pieces."

Dawson responded, "Yes, there is also a machine diagram. I need your help with the theory to energize a power cell for the device."

Nervously, Easton responded, "When can I see the rest? I must see everything!" He had forgotten about the baseball game, the beer, and even where he was. He said again, "Where is the rest? I must see everything. Are you building the laser?" His eyes were intense.

"If I let you see the rest of the material, you must stay at our compound until we finish building the machine. We are working under a short time line, and security is tight. You will not be able to leave until we finish." Dawson became serious as he took back his paper and tore the writing off of the folder where Dr. Easton had scribbled his notes.

"What's this about? This is a major breakthrough. What is the machine?" asked Dr. Easton.

"I am not sure. If you agree to work with me, you can tell no one. We will pay you well. First, you must sign a nondisclosure agreement," responded Dawson.

"Spring break starts tomorrow. I can work with you for a week," responded Dr. Easton.

"Great. Is fifty thousand dollars enough for your time?" Dawson asked while he finished his beer, tossing empty peanut shells onto the floor.

"That's a lot of money for a week's work. Yes," said Dr. Easton.

"Meet me at the train station in the morning at six. I will pick you up. Don't bring anything but clothes for the week, no computers or mobile phones. Tell no one about this project." Dawson gathered up his things and shook Easton's hand. He left the bar, but one of Dawson's men stayed behind to follow the doctor until they met in the morning.

Dr. Easton arrived at the train station, anxious to see the rest of the formula. He had spent the early part of his career researching a similar theory, but he was never able to complete it. He sat on the train platform with nervous anticipation of what the week would bring.

Dawson walked up behind him, tapped his shoulder, and said, "It's time to go."

Easton was startled out of his daydream. He replied, "It's you. I am so excited. I couldn't sleep last night."

"I am looking forward to working with you too, Doctor. The vehicle is over there by the shuttle shelter. We are double-parked, so we must hurry," said Dawson while pointing the way and gathering Dr. Easton's bag.

"I thought we were taking the train to your lab. Why are we driving?" Easton asked, anxiously following Dawson to the parking lot.

"It's just a security protocol. Nothing to worry about. We will be there in a few hours, but first we need you to sign some documents and prepare you for the upcoming week," explained Dawson as he opened the door to the van.

"I just want to know what we are doing," Easton replied nervously.

The driver pulled away from the curb while Dawson and Dr. Easton settled in the seating area in the rear of the van. The van was customized for travel, with captain's chairs and a small table for a traveling guest. Dawson closed the privacy door between the front seats and the rear of the van. He opened his folder, produced a document, and said, "This is the nondisclosure agreement we discussed yesterday. You must sign this document before we leave the city, otherwise the driver will drop you off wherever you desire. You'll see the amount we agreed on for your week's work. The fifty thousand dollars is highlighted in paragraph three. Take a moment to review the document and sign on the bottom of page three."

Dr. Easton scanned the document then said, "Everything appears to be in order. But what is this hypnosis clause at the bottom of page two?"

"If you agree to the terms of the agreement and the compensation, we will use hypnosis to prevent you from remembering the work performed under this contract," Dawson replied calmly then asked the doctor if he wanted a cold drink from the refrigerator.

Stunned, Easton pushed the papers away and folded his arms. He said, "I will not let you poke around my mind for any price. Who are you people?"

Dawson tapped on the door, then asked the driver to turn around and go back to the train station. He said, "I understand your concern. This is a harmless hypnotic procedure that professionals use to help people stop smoking or lose weight. This is not mind control. If you do not want to continue, we will drop you back at the station."

"I'm not comfortable with hypnosis. Did you say it is done to lose weight?" replied Easton.

"Yes, it's very effective," responded Dawson as he took a sip from his drink.

"I've been trying to lose twenty pounds for the last ten years with no success. I don't know…" Easton picked up the document to read the contract again.

The driver announced, "Sir, we are at the train station. Where do you want to stop?"

Dawson looked at Dr. Easton and asked, "What's your decision?"

"Will I remember anything from the work I perform this week?" Easton asked with sweat rolling down his cheek.

"It's difficult to say. Everyone is different. I will include a suggestion for your weight loss goal in the hypnosis session if you agree to go forward," responded Dawson.

A car behind the van started blowing its horn, anxious for the van to move from the passenger drop-off zone. Dawson asked, "Are we leaving you here?"

"No, I will sign the contract. Let's go."

Dr. Easton signed the contract and passed it back to Dawson. Dawson said, "Don't worry, this is a safe procedure, you'll see. Trust me." He handed the professor a gold coin.

Dawson placed the coin in Dr. Easton's hand and asked him to focus on the shiny object. Dawson took the coin back, waved it in the air before the doctor's eyes, and then said, "Your eyes are getting heavy..."

CHAPTER 4

A black taxi stopped abruptly in front of a coffee shop near the port in Calais, France. The passenger paid the driver and quickly exited the vehicle without looking back. He faded into a group of pedestrians walking by. The passenger was a thin tall man in a dark trench coat and a hat. The hat he wore looked similar to the one worn by Humphrey Bogart in the 1940 era movie *Casablanca*. His gray hat with a black band was in style in the forties and fifties, but not today. The man seemed out of place among the people who passed him by on the street. His pale face was badly in need of a shave. However, his blandness made him easily forgettable.

A few blocks away in a small hotel, Thomas Jet had spent a few weeks healing from his surgery. That morning he made contact with the Brotherhood's command ship, the *Scorpion*, which was anchored in the harbor. Thomas packed his bag and took one final look in the mirror before leaving the room. The person peering back at him was not the Thomas he remembered from Chicago who had started this journey, but instead he was Jessie's son from the Congo. Growing up and into adulthood, Thomas did not know who his real father was until Dr. Oble planted the seed of doubt in his mind. Discovering the fact that his uncle Jessie was really his father had changed his life. Thomas thought, *Let's get this new life on the road.*

Thomas grabbed his bag and jogged down three flights of stairs to the front desk to check out of the hotel. The woman at the front desk closed out his bill after receiving his cash and then pointed across the room. In English tinged with a French accent, she said, "Monsieur, the man in the coffee lounge is looking for someone. He has been waiting about an hour, watching all the guests as they check out. You asked me to let you know if I saw anyone acting this way, right?"

Thomas nodded and took his change. He exited the hotel through the side door to the alley to avoid the stranger. Safely outside, he walked around to the street in front of the hotel. He peered through the window to get a good look at his unwelcome visitor. The stranger, dressed in a hat and coat, looked somewhat familiar to him but not enough to be recognized. He turned to leave and then stopped when a voice in the back of his mind said, "Thomas, stop running. Face life head on. See what he wants with you." Reluctantly, Thomas heeded his instincts. He opened the door to the hotel and greeted the stranger.

"Are you looking for me? How can I help you?" asked Thomas, looking suspiciously at the man.

"I have something from Maalik. Did you know him? I have traveled a great distance," announced the stranger.

"Who are you? I know no Maalik," responded Thomas, thinking the man was an IBC agent, or worse, CIA.

The International Bureau of Commerce (IBC) was an organization focused on securing mineral rights in developing countries. Their agents were ex-CIA, British MI6, and mercenaries engaged in espionage to gain the advantage to secure control of diamonds, gold, oil, and other resources for their clients.

The stranger reached in his pocket and presented a tiny cracked vase. Maalik had carried the small vase with him the last few months of his life. Thomas recognized the ancient object immediately. The little vase was as old as the Brotherhood. The founders had broken and mended it as a symbol of the purpose of the organization. Thomas was shocked to see the stranger with it. He knew Maalik was the last person to have it. Maalik would never voluntarily give the miniature vase to a stranger. Thomas was now even more suspicious of the pale man.

The man responded, "Maalik's voice woke me two days ago and urged me to come to this place and bring this vase. I was not sure who I was looking for."

"Did you murder Maalik?" Thomas raised his voice to a loud whisper, reaching into his pocket for his gun, but not pulling it out.

"No, I was with Maalik when several masked men attacked us and took him away. It was dark, but they looked like ex-military. Maalik had told me he felt he was being followed. He suspected IBC agents, but he was not sure. We fought, but we were outnumbered. They left me for dead." He removed his hat to show Thomas the scars from the fight hidden underneath. "This vase was found near my body when the police found me and carried me to the hospital. Maalik's thoughts guided me to you. Please take this. I am sure he wanted you to have it," the stranger explained in a hoarse, raspy voice with tears in his eyes.

Still suspicious, Thomas softened and asked, "Who are you?"

"I was sent as an emissary to your Brotherhood thirty years ago. Our brethren split from the Knights Templar in Iberia, before it became Spain. Our founders took a poverty oath to help only the poor. Our monastery is located near Lourdes, France, in the foothills of the Pyrenees Mountains. We have few resources, but we share information with those of like minds. When we were attacked a few months ago, I was not sure if I was the target or Maalik, but when he was dragged away, I knew. I was sent to warn Maalik of an imminent threat, but we were attacked before we could talk. Names are dangerous. Maalik called me Emissary."

Thomas took the small vase and examined it; then he put it away in his pocket. "What sort of threat are we talking about?"

"One of our brethren is missing. His last report included information about a cult and rumors of a new kingdom called New Elysium. He was engaged in mission work in a small village near Granada, Spain. There were rumors and grumblings from the locals about a nearby research facility. Our brother is feared dead. Furthermore, in the desert near Morocco, there were mysterious deaths reported for no apparent cause. At night, people say truck convoys removed the dead without giving the families any information on where the bodies were taken. It could be a new plague," whispered the stranger while taking the last sip from his coffee.

"Why are you telling me?" asked Thomas, looking around for others who might be watching.

"You Americans are new to this life. We view your African Brotherhood as a fifth column working in Africa to make right the evil things that have been done to the continent over the centuries. If these rumors about a new kingdom called New Elysium are true, all of Africa, and maybe the rest of the world is at risk. There is talk of a new world order, like when the world was at war with Germany." The stranger stood and extended his hand to Thomas.

Reluctantly, Thomas nodded and shook his hand. "Thanks for returning the vase. I will consider what you told me, but frankly, you have not given me much to go on."

"That's all we know. But with Maalik now dead, I had no one else to tell. Stay safe." The man handed Thomas a folded piece of paper then departed. Thomas watched the man walk past the hotel window thinking, *He looks like he stepped out of the past. His hands were ice cold. Is this what Maalik's world was like?*

Thomas opened the folded paper and mumbled, "More coded messages to unscramble." He placed the paper in his pocket next to the vase and made his way to the harbor, watching his surroundings to determine if he was being followed. After dark, he boarded a small boat for the short trip to the *Scorpion*. Thomas was troubled by the visit from the stranger and his warning of an eminent threat. He thought about Maalik and the little vase now in his possession. He wondered if he was up to the challenge to lead the Brotherhood. The splashing of waves on the little boat had his mind thinking back to sailing on Lake

Michigan and living a simpler life as an investment banker in Chicago.

From the distance, the ship's profile appeared harmless, with its masts extended high above the ship. The trawler, with its huge nets, was designed for efficient fishing. The hull was painted black with a red stripe just above the waterline. The rest of the ship was painted gray with black trim to highlight the rails. The smell of fish welcomed Thomas aboard. The crew worked to load cargo as he climbed the stairs to the wheelhouse. The ship functioned as a working fishing ship in order to achieve his goal of stealth.

Upon boarding the ship, the security chief approached Thomas with an electronic scanner to scan the microchip implant in his arm. The screen flashed when it read the chip, then a picture of Thomas before the plastic surgery filled the screen. He snapped a new picture for the database then welcomed Thomas aboard. The news quickly spread on the ship of Thomas's return with his new appearance. Down below was where the operations of the Brotherhood's intelligence network hummed with activity. When Thomas entered the control room, there was a slight pause and then everyone went back to work. He smiled and then walked down the hall to his office. Hours later, the ship raised anchor en route to Morocco.

CHAPTER 5

The pilot radioed the plane's arrival in Egypt. "We are making our final approach, Alexandria Tower."

The air traffic controller responded, "C9A009 proceed to runway A12 west. You are cleared for landing. Proceed to Terminal F C-hanger."

The pilot announced to his lone passenger, "Fasten your seat belt." The sleek Gulfstream G650 circled the airport, preparing to land.

Miss Erd had not planned to deplane in Alexandria. This was only a scheduled refueling stop. However, a warning light was flashing on the control panel, which worried the pilot. Erd agreed to a two-hour layover to allow the maintenance crew to check out the warning light and complete the refueling process. Erd's mind wandered back to a month earlier when she traveled to New Jersey to deliver a precious package. It had pained her to part with the ancient dagger, which had been recovered from the ruins of Great Zimbabwe. The gem-studded knife had become a part of her. She was obsessed with finding its secrets but had no success. Thomas Jet had convinced Erd that Brother Dawson was the one qualified to analyze the dagger to find the answers they needed.

Erd lingered on the plane to gather her things. The crew offered to help her, but she ignored them. Halfway down the stairs, she noticed the pilot's body on the floor of the hanger. The zip of silencer bullets suddenly rang through the hanger bay. Erd's heart thumped as she crouched down on the steps, trying to avoid a line of bullets that ripped through the side of the plane. Four men wearing masks appeared from behind a storage rack, firing their weapons in the air. The copilot was shot while trying to protect Erd. His body tumbled down the stairs in front of her, onto the concrete floor. The flight attendant stood shaking in front of the plane with her hands in the air, tears running down her face.

Stunned, Erd screamed, "Stop firing. We are unarmed!"

One gunman grabbed Erd by the hair and dragged her to stand next to the flight attendant. She trembled, watching the leader of the group approach her. Erd shouted, "You cowards cover your faces to kill the innocent. What do you want?"

The man moved closer to her, standing less than a foot away. Towering over her small frame, he slapped Erd's face, knocking her to the ground. He pulled her petite body up by her hair and grunted while breathing down her neck. "You are the one called Erd, yes?"

Erd did not respond.

He said, "Oh, now you have no words for me. We know who you are Miss Oshalo Seehwo Erd. Before we are through, we will have all of your words." He held his gun to the head of the flight attendant next to her and fired. Pieces of brain and skull splattered onto Erd's face and clothing. Two other men grabbed Erd by the arms while the leader retrieved a large syringe from his backpack. He injected a green substance into her neck. Her body fell limp on the concrete floor.

Only fifteen minutes had passed. The four dead bodies were left where they fell. Erd's limp body was thrown into a large suitcase and carried to a waiting cargo plane. Once on the plane, Erd was strapped in a chair with an IV in her arm. Her clothes were removed and discarded, replaced with a flight suit.

On the radio was the voice of Stark. "Good job. There will be a bonus for you when you deliver the package. You must at all times keep her sedated. She has a unique psychic ability to read thoughts and mental impressions. Keep your masks on until you reach the rendezvous. Do not underestimate her."

"This is a lot of trouble for a tiny woman. No worries, we have the IV flowing the fluid into her veins. We removed a microchip capsule from under her skin. She is still unconscious," responded the man in English with a thick Russian accent.

"Do not damage her. I want her unharmed," shouted Stark.

"Yes, sir. Understood." The radio went silent.

CHAPTER 6

An enormous dust storm from the Sahara Desert swept south, covering everything in its path with a thick blanket of sand. Street traffic came to an abrupt halt, forcing people in the marketplace to run for cover. Within seconds, the city appeared deserted. A black Jeep Cherokee stopped in front of a mud and stone structure. The radio played local music. The broadcast was interrupted with an announcer saying, "Breaking news, an entire village in the desert is missing! Hundreds feared dead! The United Nations is investigating with local authorities!" The radio then went back to regular programming.

Jamal made several attempts to get out of the vehicle, but the force of the violent wind made him wait until the storm subsided. He was anxious to stretch his long legs after the hour-long ride from the airport. His chestnut brown skin did not mind the brutal heat of the desert sun. However, he wore his trademark cap to keep the sun out of his eyes. Months earlier, Erd's talk of Timbuktu and the Mali kingdom had captured Jamal's imagination. He wanted to see Timbuktu for himself.

Thomas Jet had asked Jamal and Zek to travel to Timbuktu in Mali, the center of learning in the former ancient kingdom, after a digital sketch of a map based on the arrangement of blue diamonds found in Belize caused a stir in the Brotherhood. The intelligence section at Cape Verde had studied the sketch to determine possible locations around the world for a similar river configuration. They determined that the Niger River in Mali was the closest match and the best place to search for possible connections to the map. Explorers and invading empires had searched for the source of Mali gold for more than one thousand years with no definitive answer of where the gold originated. This was why England named Ghana the "Gold Coast" when it was taken as a colonial possession at the turn of the twentieth century. The possibility of undiscovered gold along the Niger River intrigued the Brotherhood.

Zek was an Afro-Brazilian who became a member of the Brotherhood five years ago. Miss Erd recruited Zek on her travels in South America while searching for a lost Mali diamond treasure. He served in military intelligence in Brazil. Zek and Jamal were paired together by the Brotherhood after working in the Gulf of Mexico to recover lost treasure.

"This is not what I imagined when we were counting baskets of diamonds," said Jamal, standing outside the decaying building. "I imagined castles and stuff with all that gold, not a city of mud and bricks. They should be living large here. What happened?"

"The Mali Empire, just like the Roman Empire, is no more. Nothing is forever. If you go to old Rome, all you find are old stones and ruins," responded Zek.

"Yeah, I see your point," responded Jamal. "My empire back in Houston is gone too."

Zek laughed. "Yeah right. Let's get to work. We have only a few hours to do some research before we return to Accra."

The guide walked ahead into the ancient building. He said, "This place is the library where maps of desert and river routes are kept. The river has changed much over the past centuries. This building is over eight hundred years old. Most caravans that crossed the Sahara stopped here for updated maps for the region." He opened the door, and they walked through a narrow hallway to the map room.

Welcome. Are you from America? LA right?" A bearded man sitting in a chair by the door greeted the party as he looked up at Jamal's cap.

"We are from all over," said Jamal.

"I admire your Nike soft shoes. Will you sell or trade for them?" the man asked as he stood up to greet his guest.

"It depends. What do you have to trade?" Jamal smiled. He thought, *This old dude is trying to get my shoes. I just walked in the place.*

"We trade for any and everything here. This is a gold candle holder just for you." The man placed the object on the table.

"Did you say gold?"

"Yes, see very nice. Yes?"

Jamal picked up the object and inspected the bottom. He said, "Made in China. This is not real gold."

"No, I did not say it was. It's gold color. Yes? Nice. You did not think I would give you real gold for your shoes. Those shoes are not worth more than one hundred dollars US. We shop on the Internet too." The man smiled then said, "Do we have a deal?"

"Naw, no deal. I'm going to watch you. I will keep my shoes. We are here to look at maps. Can you help with that?" Jamal placed the candleholder back on the table and turned to look at Zek.

"Yes we have many maps of the Niger. What do you need?" The man opened a wide drawer and started pulling out several maps of the river.

"This is a sketch that we are trying to match up with the river," said Zek as he placed the diagram on the table.

"Interesting. I've seen this before." The man reached below to the bottom drawer to produce several smaller maps.

"Do you think this could be the Niger River?" Jamal turned the sketch around for a different view.

"You know the river is twenty-six hundred miles long. You are looking for something else." The man turned the sketch around again and said, "I think this is a stream that feeds into the river near the Guinea border." He pulled a smaller map from the stack for everyone to see. He said, "See the v-split separation at the end? This is the closest match to your sketch. It could be you are searching the wrong river; the Blue Nile in Ethiopia maybe an option."

"Great, we will start here for now. Can I purchase this map from you?" Jamal pulled a wad of money from his pocket.

"I'll trade for your shoes." The man rolled up the map and looked down at Jamal's shoes.

"Not today." Jamal peeled off two hundred dollars from his roll and nodded to the man. Zek and Jamal headed for the airport to return to Ghana.

CHAPTER 7

It had been forty-eight hours since Goode heard English other than what he could find on the television. Every TV channel was in Russian except one BBC news channel. Goode longed to speak to someone without thinking about language and translation. Of course, he could speak Russian well enough to get by. However, every moment reminded Goode that he was a stranger in a foreign land. The frigid cold and snowdrifts along the street would not bother him, if only someone would say something in English. Spring was long overdue. There were no signs of green sprouts or warm breezes, only more snow in the forecast.

He put those thoughts in the back of his mind to focus on his mission: to find a new market for the Brotherhood's diamonds. The Russian mafia had entered the diamond business twenty years ago when the Soviet Union fell apart. They had their tentacles in every facet of the business from mining, cutting, and distribution of finished stones.

The trip to Russia was just business as usual for Goode, until he got a message from Thomas Jet that Erd was missing. Three months had passed since Maalik had disappeared. Only his torso had been found in Paris. A sense of fear settled over the Brotherhood when the news spread that Erd was missing. Although they would not admit it, the brothers were nervous about a future without Erd, and with their new untested leader, Thomas Jet. Goode could not break from the negotiations with the

Russians to help with the search for Erd, as much as he wanted to.

Goode left his meeting early to clear his head from hearing Russians speak for hours. Returning to his hotel, he followed a cobblestone street along a canal that flowed into Neva Bay in St. Petersburg. He noticed memorial plaques and statutes for heroes from wars of the last century. The images of Stalin and Lenin were familiar to him. His mind floated, thinking of history. Finally, his mind was blank, without thoughts of negotiating points for the diamond deal or Erd's fate. There was only the sound of his footsteps and the bitter cold wind blowing through gaps in the scarf around his neck.

At the hotel, the doorman opened the door for Goode. As he entered the lobby, an attractive woman dressed in red with a fur coat on her arm approached him. She greeted him in a thick Russian accent. "Hello, sir. This is for you." The woman smiled then handed him an envelope. She did not wait for him to read the note. Instead, she walked out the door and got into a waiting car. It was strange, but everything had seemed a little odd to Goode on that trip. He went to the bar to warm up and ordered a coffee to speed up the process. He pulled off his gloves, then the coat, and used his coffee to warm his hands. He opened the envelope. Inside was a strand of hair and a note: *We have the woman called Erd. If you want to see her alive again, do as we say. You will receive instructions within the next twenty-four hours.*

Goode sipped his coffee and thought, *Could this be coming from the Russians or the International Bureau of Commerce.*

The IBC could have found out the Brotherhood recovered the diamonds from Belize and are now seeking to remove them from the market. On the other hand, the Russians may be trying to leverage us for a better price. He stopped thinking and quickly looked around the bar. No one seemed particularly interested in him, but he knew they were watching.

Goode calmed down and finished his coffee, then stopped by the business center to check for a package he was expecting. The clerk handed him a small box with international labels on the front. Goode slipped the package in his coat pocket. He did not go to his room. Instead, he had the doorman call him a taxi. The doorman asked for the address for his destination. Goode murmured, "The Equinox."

Puzzled, the doorman closed the car door and the taxi disappeared into the night.

* * * * *

Three men dressed in black paced the floor, waiting. They never looked at each other. Instead, the men just walked deliberately while studying the cracks in the concrete floor. After an hour of the *tap, tap, tap* of footsteps, a gunshot rang out from behind the closed door. The men looked at each other, nodding as if that was what they were waiting for. A man staggered from the room with blood on his head and chest and then fell to the floor.

Napoli Chenko walked out behind him with a .45 automatic in his hand. He shot the man again in the back of the head. The crew knew what to do next. They covered the body with plastic and carried it out to the van parked in the alley. Napoli was the underboss of the Pensquse crime family in the Russian mafia. The tattoos on his neck and arms showed his rank in the underworld. He enjoyed personally eliminating problems, as he called them. A former KGB agent, he led by example. His crew feared him because that type of scene happened too frequently and without any notice. Privately, some thought Napoli was crazy, but no one challenged him. He had spies everywhere. Napoli indirectly controlled the diamond business in St. Petersburg. Diamond cutters and wholesalers paid him protection money. He got the pick of the best stones. The mafia had other businesses as well, including racketeering, gambling, and prostitution. The diamond trade was Napoli's interest. He wore a five-carat, blue diamond pinky ring as his new trademark. No large diamond transaction in St. Petersburg occurred without his knowledge.

CHAPTER 8

Stark Phillips was a former Soviet KGB agent who had defected to the West. He was granted a new identity in exchange for secrets about the former Soviet Union. He worked for British Intelligence MI6—the counterintelligence section. Unknown to MI6, Stark was a double agent working for the KGB. When the cold war ended, Stark went to work for the IBC, but maintained his undercover status with the KGB. Stark admired the IBC's ruthlessness. It reminded him of the KGB before Glasnost, the Russian policy that called for increased openness and transparency in government that was the precursor to the breakup of the Soviet Union. Banister Lofton recruited Stark to the search for the mythical dagger now in the Brotherhood's possession.

Lofton believed in the existence of the dagger. He became obsessed with the object. While seizing on every bit of information on its origin, he stumbled onto an ancient Sanskrit document reported to have been found in an obscure Muslim mosque in Morocco. The script described a Moorish dagger that contained secret technology that would have been impossible to exist for the period. The discovery of the Antikythera, an ancient Greek mechanical computer, was validation for Lofton that unknown technology was still yet undiscovered.

Lofton's research revealed that the Moors had amassed vast libraries that contained works of the Romans, Greeks, and even the ancient Egyptians. This confirmed his suspicions that the dagger may contain previously lost technology, such as the Antikythera. Moorish libraries included books on mathematics, optics, physics, mechanics, navigation, and numerous other disciplines. Researchers were dispatched to Morocco to search Moorish archives for information on the dagger's origin. Lofton, a Spanish billionaire arms dealer, funded Stark's operations with the hopes of weaponizing the power of the dagger. The retrieval of the dagger in Zimbabwe by the Brotherhood was the last thing Frederick Eddington, the former head of the IBC, who was obsessed with finding lost African treasure, spoke of before his death. Now the quest for the dagger was Lofton's single focus.

Stark's benefactor, Banister Lofton, was a recluse, rarely seen in public. The only published picture of him was from his teenage years when he was playing tennis. When the media ran a story about his empire, a faded sixty-year-old picture was the sole image of the billionaire arms dealer. Even Stark did not know what Lofton looked like. His only contact with the man was through an envoy. The absence of his investor, at one point, emboldened Stark to ridicule the man who provided him with endless resources for the search of phantom artifacts like the dagger. The private jokes and heckles ended when Stark's wife was found severed nearly in half, from her neck through her stomach, splitting her body in two. The body was found on Stark's favorite golf course with a note saying, "Here lies the wife of a man who thinks he is important."

Officials in Amsterdam found no evidence of those responsible. After the funeral, Stark received a rare call from Lofton. "My sympathy for your loss. These are times when one should choose his words wisely. You seem to have created a powerful enemy. Be careful." Stark understood the message.

Lofton's family had been in the arms business since the Middle Ages. His family held debts from France, Spain, and England for armaments for various crusade campaigns to free the holy lands from Muslim control. War was good for business. Lofton understood the importance of research and development when it came to making war. Whoever had the latest weapon had the advantage and won the spoils of war. Ultimately, Lofton's ancestors developed weapon technology for the use of gunpowder and specialized in canons. Gunpowder and canons made castles extinct as a form of control and power. When the Middle Ages were at an end, Lofton's arms business was on the winning side of the Spanish quest to build a vast empire.

As gunpowder was being lauded as the next new thing in warfare, there was an event that caused a stir when a yet unknown weapon left many astonished on the field of battle. A brilliant light flashed from a castle near the battlefield during one of many of the Spanish skirmishes with the Moors in fourteenth century Spain. The bright light left the Spanish soldiers blinded until an energy wave pushed them back to the river. The weapon was never used again. Eventually, the Moors surrendered.

Almost everyone forgot about the blinding light and the energy wave except Lofton's ancestor. The elder Lofton had been on the battlefield and had felt the wave pulse that pushed the attackers across the river. The mysterious weapon was a thing of legend around the Lofton dinner table for centuries. The stories changed over the years. However, in private conversations when family elders gathered, the tone turned ominously serious with the mention of the portentous Moorish weapon.

Banister discovered an ancient diary forty years ago while overseeing a remodeling project of the family estate located near Seville, Spain. His ancestor had written in detail about a mysterious weapon. The last entry on the fading pages noted that if the weapon ever reemerged, the balance of power would forever be changed. The entry was dated January 2, 1576. Banister read the diary entry and was puzzled by the observation in the age of great sailing ships and Spanish armada firepower. *How could anyone stand up to Spain's power then?* he thought.

Currently, Lofton Industries built jet fighters, battle cruisers, and submarines. The research and development department continuously searched for an edge for the next best weapon. Lofton Industries was the preferred provider of arms for Frederick Eddington and the IBC for sponsored conflicts in Africa and other hot spots around the world.

CHAPTER 9

A picturesque scene greeted the travelers on the road to Cape Coast in Ghana. The horizon was dotted with fishing boats adorned with colorful red, yellow, and white sails. A strong easterly breeze pushed the small fishing boats out to sea. Jamal pointed at several women balancing baskets filled with dried smoked fish on their heads. The driver pulled over onto the curb and announced, "I'm hungry. I will be back in a few minutes." He crossed the street to speak to one of the women who had fish for sale. The two of them stood in the street, negotiating the price. The man returned to the car, smiling, with a brown paper bag full of smoked dried fish. He started eating and passed the bag to Jamal saying, "You are in for a treat. Try it. It's good and fresh."

Jamal glanced back at Zek, wondering if the fish was safe to eat, then took a small bite. "Not bad," he said, passing the bag to Zek. The three men feasted until all the fish were gone.

"Now that's a different kind of fast food. In Ghana, they've probably been doing this hundreds of years before KFC started its chicken business," said Jamal. Everyone laughed as the car turned back on the road to continue the journey to the slave castle.

"Yes, Ghanaians have enjoyed smoked fish for a long time," the driver said with a grin as he looked back at Jamal through the rearview mirror.

The car came to a stop in front of a huge stone structure. Several children gathered around the van, hoping to sell trinkets for coins from the tourists' pockets. Jamal and Zek strolled past the children to the ramp to tour the oldest slave castle in Ghana. For Jamal, it was surreal to see the historic slave castle, Elmina, built in 1482 by the Portuguese. The first European slave- trading post built in sub-Saharan Africa. Portugal and Spain are responsible for developing the slave trade that was focused on shipping Africans to the Americas. The slavery until death model they perfected in South America and the Caribbean was followed by the British, French, and others. The final defeat of the Moors was the same year that Christopher Columbus discovered America.

How can something so evil, which is responsible for the suffering of Africans, be surrounded by a picturesque fishing village? Jamal thought.

Walking up the ramp, Zek felt a strange twinge in his arm. His mood changed to somber as he began thinking about the purpose of the castle. He finally said, "Millions of Africans passed through these doors for almost four hundred years."

A young college student, who worked as the tour guide, greeted the two men and proceeded to explain the history of the castle. Jamal listened, but his mind was troubled by Zek's comment. As Jamal walked behind Zek and the guide, he took a wrong turn and became separated from them. In the darkness, Jamal ran to catch up, and hit his head on the low ceiling arch of a slave dungeon. His body lay motionless on the ground, and he was unconscious until he felt a sharp pain across his back. Again, the pain came. It felt like a whip.

This is impossible, he thought.

He opened his eyes and saw standing over him a white man with a whip, urging him to get up.

"Move forward, get up, move forward."

With every word, Jamal felt another lash across his back. Blood ran freely onto the floor. He could not move, though he wanted to. He discovered he was shackled to five other men. When Jamal fell, everyone went down. One man was too weak to get up. With another lash to Jamal's back, the man said, "Pick him up or you will die where he fell."

The whip claimed another slice of Jamal's back until he picked up the man. His tethered group finally moved forward to allow a long line of bound men into the dungeon. Jamal counted one hundred men and then stopped when the room became cramped. The air was thick with sweat and misery.

Jamal thought, *I need to wake up! This dream feels too real.* He felt his back. Deep gashes were cut into his skin. Blood puddled on the floor behind him. He called out, "Zek, where are you? Come get me. Wake me up. Get me out of here!"

The man with the whip came back and struck him across the face with the handle, knocking his head to the floor. After a few minutes, Jamal woke up. Zek was standing over him with a bottle of water. He said, "Are you ok? I heard you call for us. We were looking for you. You must have hit your head. Your head is bleeding."

"Yeah, something like that." Jamal did not say anything else. He felt his back and looked around the dungeon. The blood was gone. He was alone with Zek and the guide. The smell was still there. He said, "I will tell you later." Jamal stood up and drank some water while rubbing his head.

After touring the slave castle, Jamal looked over a wall that overlooked the ocean and saw the doorway they called the "Door of No Return." He said, "The last sight enslaved Africans would see would be the endless ocean for a long journey to the unknown. It had to be scary to be shackled, beaten, and taken to who knows where. Black folks have been through hell." Jamal shook his head as he thought about what happened to him in the dungeon.

Seeing the vibrant fishing village on the other side of the wall, Zek said, "Something about this seems out of place. Inside these walls, I can smell death and humanity. I feel the pain of my brothers and sisters chained in slavery. However, outside life goes on."

Jamal responded, "Yes. I see your point, but life does go on. The people on the other side of the wall were not enslaved, so the connection is different. Their lives went on, where ours in the Americas changed forever. You cannot go back to the beginning. You must move forward from wherever you are."

Back at the car, Zek got emotional. "I hope the Brotherhood is going to fix this, because I'm not feeling this right now. I'm not sure of how welcome I feel in Africa after seeing this."

"Hey, brother, Africa is more complex than that. Remember, the prophecy warned about the invasion, slavery, and millions dead...but no one listened. The old king foresaw all of this one thousand years ago. Our job is to prepare for the rebirth of the continent. All Africans have suffered." Jamal patted Zek on the shoulder. He pulled out his iPod and plugged it in the car stereo. An old-school song from James Brown came on. Jamal started rocking and singing along, "Get ready for the big payback..."

Zek joined in, and the three men sang along with James Brown's greatest hits for the next few hours of the ride back to Accra.

* * * * *

At the hotel in Accra, Jamal received a message from Thomas to contact Goode. When Jamal called Goode, he heard the news about Erd's disappearance and the note Goode had received hours earlier. Goode gave Jamal the latest intelligence on possible locations where Erd could be held.

"Erd was taken in Alexandria, Egypt. They got her out of the country by air. We think she is somewhere in the Mediterranean," Goode said.

"Has she tried to contact you with her mind link?"

"No, they probably have her drugged. She is still alive. I can feel her presence."

"I am not going to sit around waiting by the phone. Zek and I are on the next thing smoking to Alexandria. We will follow the trail from there," said Jamal while packing his bag.

Goode knew nothing he could say would stop Jamal. He said, "Okay, Jamal, start at the Borg El Arab Airport, Terminal F at the security office. Airport police found four bodies, the plane crew, and a mechanic in the terminal building. Be discreet. Let Zek handle the police. Brother, you know you don't do well with them."

"All right, I got this. Zek will ride shotgun with me. I will check in when we arrive."

Zek met Jamal in the hotel lobby and they took a taxi to the airport. It had been four hours since Erd last made contact with Thomas.

CHAPTER 10

Sunswept beaches of Gran Canaria in the Canary Islands served as a welcome retreat for Jack Regis and Theo. Jack Regis was an ex-CIA agent and former military intelligence officer who served with Thomas Jet in the army. Thomas and Jack had been lifelong friends. Miss Erd, the psychic leader within the Brotherhood, had discovered that Jack Regis was a descendant of one the founders of the Brotherhood. Although Jack acknowledged a connection to the Brotherhood, he did not believe he was a descendant of the group's founder. Theo was a teenager from Zimbabwe whom Jack took responsibility for after it was determined that it would be dangerous for the boy to return to his home. Theo helped the Brotherhood thwart a terrorist attack in Zimbabwe.

The trip to the island was an opportunity for the two men to recharge from their adventure in South Africa. It was too soon for Jack to consider a return to the States. He had not determined what to do with Theo, but now he had become fond of him. Jack could not think of parting with his young protégé. Miss Erd had encouraged Jack to take Theo with him to keep him safe. Her word was enough to welcome the young man into the ancient organization. *Theo said his parents died when he was a child, but who is he really?* thought Jack. Jack suspected Erd knew more about Theo than she was telling him.

He considered adoption or legal guardianship as an option, but that could make Theo a target. It was best to keep things simple. Their doctored traveling documents, a passport and birth certificate provided by the Brotherhood, showed Jack as Theo's father, so there was no need to do more. Theo learned to swim at the resort pool. His long braided hair enticed young girls to follow him around in the market place. Theo was having the time of his life until he noticed Jack was packing and preparing for a trip.

Jack had received an urgent message from Thomas asking him to meet him in Casablanca. The message didn't say what had happened, but Jack knew Thomas had to be in trouble. "I will be leaving this afternoon, heading to Morocco for a few days. You will be fine here while I'm gone. Remember what I told you about strangers. Never use your real name and follow the script I gave you on your past," Jack announced.

Theo responded, "Don't worry about me. I know how to be a secret agent." He smiled and then got serious. "Is it nearing the time for us to leave the island?"

"Yes," Jack pulled his backpack onto his shoulder. "We will be leaving in a few weeks."

"I will miss this place. I was hoping this could be home," Theo said as he sat at the bar, sadly looking through pictures on his phone.

"Cheer up," said Jack. "You have at least a few more weeks before we leave, so enjoy yourself."

Theo walked Jack to the car and gave him a hug. He said, "No problem, I know the move will be for the best. Go well, Jack."

In the car, looking out the rearview mirror, Jack thought about Theo and everything that had happened over the last four months. It seemed like a lifetime ago. Thomas had replaced Maalik as the head of intelligence for the Brotherhood.

I promised to help Thomas, Jack thought as he boarded the plane.

* * * * *

Jack's flight arrived late at Casablanca International Airport. As he exited the gate, for a brief moment, Jack thought he saw his former boss from the CIA, JB Sutton. However, the man quickly vanished from view. Jack shook his head, walked for a few minutes, and then turned around. He felt as if he were being followed. The hair on the back of his neck tingled. He sensed something was off. He went into the restroom where he waited for the unwanted company. Five minutes passed and no one entered. But then, there he was.

"What are you doing here?" questioned Jack.

"I could ask you the same thing, but you won't tell me the truth," responded JB.

"Are you following me?"

"Yes and no."

"Tell me the yes part," said Jack.

"Waiting to board my flight, I saw you at the gate. You disappeared, so I decided to follow you. How's that for an answer?"

"I guess that's the best I am going to get," Jack replied.

"Yes, sorry. You know how it is. We can only say so much. Your friend is in trouble. She may be dead. All that blood is not a good sign," mumbled JB while checking his watch. "I am going to miss my flight."

"What and who are you talking about? What blood? Where?" questioned Jack.

"Oh, you don't know. Your folks are slipping. You will find out soon enough. It's good to see you. I decided to stay on the job a little while longer. Our folks are still looking for you, so watch your back. There's a rumor about diamonds."

"What are you talking about?" Jack grabbed JB's shoulder.

"If you need to contact me, call me at the bathhouse in Istanbul. You remember the place, right?" JB walked toward the door, hurrying to catch his flight.

Jack ran to catch up with him. "Yeah, yeah, I remember. JB, you can contact me at this number, text only," Jack whispered as he scribbled the number on a piece of paper. He stuffed the number in JB's pocket as they left the restroom. He thought, *Who is in trouble? Why was JB in Morocco?*

Jack exited the airport, looking for Thomas, but there was no sight of him. He started to go back in the airport terminal when a porter stopped him and directed him toward a waiting car. Inside the car, he found Thomas sitting in the back, wearing dark glasses and what looked like a fake nose and chin, along with a thick beard. His arms and chest were enlarged with muscle. Startled, Jack said, "I didn't recognize you. What did you do?" Jack had not seen Thomas since he'd had the plastic surgery performed on his face in Paris.

Thomas ignored Jack's question and proceeded to talk about the weather. Finally, he said, "Jack, I am not the same person, my friend. These changes were necessary." Nothing else was said for a few minutes. The taxi cleared the airport traffic and headed for a seaside village near Dar Bouazza.

When Jack last saw Thomas on Cape Verde, he had been amazed at how much Thomas had changed. His eyes were dark and intense. Thomas's movements were deliberate and his words measured. He was not the man he'd remembered. Jack knew something had happened to Thomas. Though Thomas explained about his father, Jessie, and the memories that were transferred to him, it was difficult for Jack to accept his old friend's appearance and that he had suddenly transformed into the elder leader of the Brotherhood's intelligence organization. And now after the plastic surgery, Thomas looked like a total stranger.

The men exited the taxi at the edge of the marketplace near the village fish auction where Thomas spotted a coffee shop. He said, "This looks like a good place to talk."

Jack, puzzled by Thomas's strange behavior, followed. After they were seated and Thomas ordered Turkish coffee, he announced, "Erd is missing. It's been eight hours. The kidnappers removed the tracking chip from her arm that we implanted as a safeguard after Maalik's death. We've lost her."

Thomas did not show any emotion, but Jack knew something was there. It strained Thomas to keep his emotions in check when it came to Erd. She was his lover, but something strange happened after the first time they made love. Erd called him her soul mate. However, because of her heightened psychic ability, her mind created a permanent link to Thomas's thoughts. He could always feel her presence, as if she had become a part of him and he a part of her. He feared showing his real feelings about her to Jack or anyone else because he needed to be the leader, not a love-struck schoolboy. Their telepathy link was constant, which was very different from his communications with the rest of the Brotherhood.

"Do you have any leads? That's what JB was talking about. My old boss from the CIA was in the airport. He said something about a lot of blood. He mentioned diamonds."

"Yeah, we sold a few diamonds. The rumors started after the sale. Erd is alive for now. A note was handed to Goode in St. Petersburg a few hours ago. It could be anyone. I thought with Eddington gone from the IBC we would have more room to operate. It could be the dagger or the diamonds they are after. Who knows?" Thomas responded in a low voice as he sipped his coffee.

"You think it's the Russians. Why would they kidnap her? Do they know about the dagger?" Jack questioned while looking around the café for suspicious characters.

"It could be anyone. The IBC had former KGB agents on their payroll or it could be a freelancer. Goode is negotiating with the Russians to cut and market some of our diamonds. They may be trying to leverage us. We don't know who is behind this," responded Thomas.

"Where is the dagger?"

"In a safe place," said Thomas. Then he added, "They know we have it, but they must also know Erd's connection to the object. We only have twenty-four hours to find her."

"Thomas, why are we here? Why aren't we out there looking for Erd?" Jack strained not to shout. He was frustrated with how calm Thomas was behaving.

"We don't know where she's being held. Jamal and Zek will follow her trail from Alexandria. Goode got a message in St. Petersburg for her ransom. Whoever we are dealing with knows a lot about us. The last message from Erd included an image of an ancient monastery located somewhere in Morocco. She must have picked up some information from her captors. This is where we will start our search," responded Thomas while unfolding a map from his pocket.

Thomas spread out a map of a mountainous area south of Casablanca. He said, "These are the Atlas Mountains. They stretch for about sixteen thousand miles, from Morocco to Tunisia. We narrowed the location to three abandoned monasteries north of Marrakesh near the high Atlas Mountains. This is Berber territory."

Jack laughed, "What do you mean Berber? I remember Erd told me I had a connection to Berbers in my family. She sent me a DNA genealogy report when I was in Joberg."

"Jack, you know you are a direct descendant of one of the founders of the Brotherhood. A Berber like you," said Thomas.

"Thomas, don't go there with that spiritual Brotherhood stuff. I am not convinced. Let's just focus on finding Erd."

"You brought it up, Jack. I arranged for a guide to meet us in Marrakech in a few hours. However, first we need to collect supplies for the trip." Thomas sipped the last of his coffee while folding up the map.

"Let's get going. Every minute is precious for finding Erd alive." Impatient, Jack stood up with his backpack on his shoulder.

Thomas led the way through the market. He said, "It is illegal for foreigners to possess fire arms in Morocco, but there is a merchant in this market who can help us."

Finally, after twenty minutes, the men arrived at an antique shop with a giant sword anchored at the front. Thomas said, "This is the place," as he pushed the door open and waded through baskets and furniture.

A woman approached Jack and said, "I've seen you before. Can I help you?"

"He would know better," Jack said as he pointed over to Thomas.

She moved closer to Jack to look at his face. She responded, "Are you sure we've never met before? Your eyes look familiar to me." The woman touched Jack's hand then walked over to ask Thomas if he needed assistance.

Thomas spoke up as she approached. "Is Amir Ransci here today?"

"Yes, he is in the back. He is my father. Do you need to speak to him?" she said, smiling at Thomas.

"Yes, he is expecting us," responded Thomas.

With her arms open, she directed the men through the shop to the back area. She knocked on a door that was bolted from the inside. "Papa, I have two men to see you."

The man pulled back the latch to see the visitors and then opened the door. The woman did not follow them into the room. The thin bearded man said, "No names, please. The less I know the better. I have what you require. Follow me."

They walked down the hallway, into a garage where an old 60's model Range Rover was parked. The vehicle was a dirty white color with rusted-out fenders. On the workbench lay a burlap sack partially covered with a blanket. Amir looked at Jack. "I have seen your eyes before. Do you have family here in Morocco?"

Jack looked at Thomas then said, "No. This is my first trip to your country."

"Well, you have a twin," responded Amir. "He has your eyes. They say we all have a twin somewhere. I hope this does not bring you trouble." The man removed the blanket and emptied the sack onto the table. He counted out an inventory of guns, a GPS, and other items. He turned around to point at the vehicle and said, "This is yours if you want it. It's only one thousand US dollars more. It runs fine. You will need something to carry away your goods."

Thomas nodded and counted out the money on the counter. An hour later, Thomas and Jack were on the road to Marrakech. Thomas said, "Do you still believe you're not part Berber?"

Jack ignored Thomas and started cleaning his gun.

CHAPTER 11

It was dark. The rain had stopped hours ago. The floor was wet from a leak in the roof. The smell of mold and mildew was thick in the air. Cobwebs accented the ceiling. Mice droppings pelted the floor from the shelf overhead. Erd was blindfolded, a rope was tied around her ankles, and her wrists were tied behind her back. The wool cloth of the blindfold was tied so tightly, her ears were numb. Erd's captors had total control of her body and mind. The gag in her mouth cut her lips. Blood began to pour freely onto the floor. The *drip*, *drip*, *drip* from the rain falling through the ceiling became her constant companion, like the tick of a clock. It was a reminder that she was alive, though she could not see her surroundings. Occasionally, a mouse would run across her leg in search of food, but she was in too much pain to worry about mice.

Every two hours, her captors would wake her for questioning: never the same questions, never the same person. She started to lose herself by freeing her mind from her body to avoid the continual torment. Ammonia was used to bring her back to consciousness so they could ask their questions. Erd was strapped in a chair and numerous needle marks on her arms revealed traces of the drugs used to weaken her mind.

Stark, who had been hired by Lofton to find the dagger, was also asking her questions. He enjoyed asking them over and over. He wanted to know what she had forgotten, even thoughts lodged in her subconscious mind. The only way to get them was to break her down to nothing, and he could then pick apart the pieces he needed from her. Her captors recorded everything, asking questions over and over until Erd could no longer resist. Erd actually thought she was already dead. Stark did not care about the Brotherhood or any other secrets she held. He wanted the dagger. He planned to trade her for the object, eventually, but before the trade, he wanted to strip everything he needed from her.

* * * * *

The Brotherhood had not solved the secret of the dagger. The mysterious artifact was valuable, with its gold, emeralds, and rubies, but the secret still had not been fully revealed. Now with Erd missing, the search for the secret intensified. The Brotherhood would never trade the dagger for Erd.

Thomas met with the elders in Paris shortly before taking over Maalik's role as head of intelligence. He asked, "Why is the dagger so important to the Brotherhood's mission in Africa? What secret could it hold that would turn Africa's fate around?"

One elder, whose voice had never been heard before, spoke. "The dagger's purpose is to meet a future threat."

Thomas sat silently for a few minutes and then said, "Future threat? What are you talking about?"

The elder responded, "The secret contained in the dagger was lost from this world. It was acquired by the king's shaman in Great Zimbabwe in the fifteenth century. Maalik's murder is an indication that the threat is imminent.

Those responsible are developing a new weapon that has the potential to devastate the continent. The dagger is the key."

Thomas said, "But what about the treasure of Great Zimbabwe? I thought that was why we were searching for the dagger."

The elder responded, "The dagger does contain the location of the gold. This is true. But the power of the dagger is what we seek."

* * * * *

Waves crashed against the thick walls of the structure. No one noticed the storm coming in from the west. The lighthouse was built one hundred years ago to withstand the harsh weather on the Mediterranean Sea. A patrol walked the perimeter of the compound. Snipers were posted in the light tower to deter unwanted visitors.

Erd was awake and talking nonstop in a childlike voice. She played with the binding on her hands and talked about her dolls. The recorder was taping every word. Her voice would change without notice into that of the adult held against her will. The drugs were working their way to unravel her will. Soon she would be broken.

Stark asked, "How old are you?"

Erd responded in an innocent voice. "Eight. How old are you?"

Stark responded, "I killed your mother and father."

Erd cried uncontrollably, unable to see due to the blindfold over her eyes. Stark laughed then said, "Don't worry little girl. Soon I will kill you too!"

Erd cried in terror until she passed out in the chair. A white-coated technician rolled her out of the room and back to the damp holding area. He dumped her on the floor.

In the next room, a woman analyzed test results from Erd's blood. She announced, "In eight hours, the patient will be completely broken."

Stark pounded the table. "That's too long. We need to move her soon."

The doctor responded, "You cannot rush the process. We are using experimental drugs. If we press too hard, she could become a vegetable. I suggest you get her off the floor and put her in a bed between treatments. She could die of pneumonia in that damp room."

Stark thought about how he would explain her death to Banister Lofton, his investor, then ordered Erd moved to a room with a bed. They put a sweatshirt on her. Stark let the doctor check her vital signs.

Afterward, Stark said, "I am not an animal. Although she means nothing to me, you are right. I need to protect our investment."

CHAPTER 12

It was 2:00 a.m. The club had just gotten its second wind. The line behind the velvet rope outside the club was halfway down the block. Music could be heard in Goode's taxi when the driver pulled up to the front door. Goode had a distinctive look. He was short and stocky but not fat. He liked hats, and that night was no different. He wore a gray fedora that matched his coat and scarf. Goode was particular about his dress. It was one of his signature trademarks.

The doorman recognized him immediately and escorted him to the VIP room upstairs. The walk to the private room required a tour of the club, going through several bar areas and along the dance floor, where scantily dressed women gyrated in erotic movements that would normally make Goode stop to admire them. That night, however, Goode made no notice of the sights along the way to the room. His mind was heavy in thought, concerned about Erd and the note he'd received at his hotel.

The package in his pocket had not been sent for this meeting, but he thought it might come in handy if he could get some answers about Erd. Goode waited patiently until the door opened and three men entered.

The leader said in a thick Russian accent, "I search you now." Goode reached in his pocket to hold the package and then stood erect to allow the search. Finding no weapons, the leader allowed Goode's entry into the room and several women joined him on the sofa.

Napoli entered the room, his eyes lit up when he saw the dapper Goode across the room. He said, "My friend, I am pleased to see you. Did they offer you something to drink?" He shouted orders to the wait staff to bring cognac, water, and coffee. Napoli had only seen Goode drink coffee, no alcohol. He valued his new friend and longed to speak in English with someone he considered his intellectual equal. After the drinks were delivered, Napoli cleared the room to speak in private.

The diamond pinky ring that Napoli wore was a prized gift from Goode, given when they first met in Hong Kong at a diamond broker conference. The blue diamond was brilliant and flawless. Goode had the ring made for himself, but Napoli had admired the ring so much that Goode took the ring off his finger and gave it to him as a parting gift. No one had ever given Napoli a gift of that value before, expecting nothing in return. Since then, Goode always had an open invitation to Napoli's club, the Equinox, whenever he was in St. Petersburg.

Goode did not know Napoli was the under boss of the Penquse crime family. He assumed he was connected to the Russian mafia but did not know how. Goode had come that night looking for help with finding out who was behind the note concerning Erd's disappearance.

"My friend, I received this note a few hours ago concerning a colleague who I fear is in danger. I thought I could seek your help to determine the source of the trouble. I have not contacted the authorities," said Goode.

Napoli read the note and asked Goode to describe who delivered the message. He said, "This strand of hair is the only proof they provided?"

Goode said, "Yes. However, I confirmed she has been missing for over eight hours. I think this may be credible."

Napoli said, "Do you think the Russian mafia is involved?"

"I don't know. I cannot assume anything," responded Goode.

"I can tell you, if my organization had done this, we would have sent a finger or an ear with the note." Napoli stood up and started pacing the floor. He asked, "Do you have enemies here?"

Goode responded, "One does not need enemies to receive threats. I deal in the diamond trade, so anything is possible."

Napoli pulled out his phone. Speaking in Russian, he called several numbers and asked questions about Goode's hotel. He had his men go and question the hotel doorman.

After thirty minutes, Napoli came back to the room. He said, "My friend, I think your trouble is coming from some of the pigs I used to work for in the government. One of my guys identified the car that picked up the lady who delivered this note as being registered to these people. They are very dangerous—no honor, just greedy bureaucrats. They work for the government and do business on the side. You did right by not contacting the police. They may only be the messenger."

Goode poured some cognac into his coffee cup. He said, "Can you help with this thing?"

Napoli poured himself another drink and then said, "We need vodka to discuss serious business!" He yelled for the waiter to bring vodka. Moments later, the bottle and two glasses arrived. Napoli took off his pinky ring and showed it to his crew, saying, "This man is my friend. Let no harm come to him." He ordered them out of the room again.

Napoli poured a glass half-full of vodka for himself and Goode. "We drink to friendship and dead strangers," He said with a smile and then drank his glass empty. He watched for Goode to complete his.

Once the last of the vodka was gone, Napoli said, "We need to watch and wait to see who has your friend. You go back to your hotel, continue your business here, and let me follow up with some of my contacts. I will contact you in the morning."

Goode was unsteady when he stood to leave, after drinking the vodka and cognac. He embraced Napoli to prepare to leave. At that moment, Napoli gave him a small caliber revolver that he took from his jacket pocket. He said, "You like to walk our historic streets alone. You should have this little friend with you on your strolls. This is my country. I love it, but it can be dangerous too."

Goode accepted the gift and left the club in a waiting taxi.

CHAPTER 13

After paying the last toll before entering the historic city of Marrakesh, Thomas said, "I expected a dusty crumbling roadway. We made good time…only two hours. Our guide should be waiting near a fruit stand at the exit."

Jack finished inspecting the gear they had purchased from Amir. He handed Thomas a .38 revolver. He kept the 9mm automatic for himself. The rest of the stuff he transferred to their backpacks.

"Thomas, you remember how to fire this thing, right?" Jack grinned while he put a clip in his gun.

"I see you kept the best piece for yourself," responded Thomas after putting his gun in his waistband.

"I have seniority. The hardware we purchased from Amir was pretty beaten up. I cleaned up the weapons as much as I could." Jack scanned the roadway, looking for the rendezvous location. He pointed to the left of a fruit stand. Thomas pulled the Range Rover onto the dirt road that ran behind the market and parked in the shade. They sat for a few minutes, watching the patrons pick through fruit.

"Enough, I'm hungry," Jack said with a grunt then got out of the vehicle. Thomas followed.

Eating figs, dates, and fresh melon slices refreshed the travelers. Jack purchased water and dried meat, then started smiling as he thought about Theo and their adventure in Zimbabwe. He said, "Theo would fit right in with us here. He's pretty tough."

"It's too dangerous. I sent someone to Gran Canary to watch over him." Thomas threw a date pit into the brush and grabbed another one to eat.

"Thanks, I was worried about him," Jack responded as he loaded his backpack with water.

"We think a lot of Theo." Thomas pointed across the road to a man approaching on foot.

"He could be our guide," said Jack.

"I think so. He looks the part," answered Thomas.

Dressed in a brown gandora and white turban, the stranger said, "Peace be with you, brother. I am Salman. We must leave quickly. It will be dark soon. Do you have transportation?"

Thomas pointed over to the underbrush where the Range Rover was parked and then he introduced Jack.

"You speak excellent English," responded Jack, looking suspiciously at the bearded man.

"Thanks, I went to UCLA. I've been back home for fifteen years now. Are you ready to go?" Salman hurried to the car. "We must reach the mountains before dark. The roads are not good. Do you mind if I drive?"

Thomas looked at Jack and then tossed Salman the keys.

"We need to go to the Bailiff Monastery first," Salman said. "It has been deserted for over fifty years…since the French left. It was a mosque before they converted it to a monastery. Based on the description you gave us, this one may be what you are looking for. It is a historic site, over twelve hundred years old. A permit is required to visit, but if we go tonight, we can avoid the check point." Salman looked back at Jack then said, "Do you have family in Marrakech? I've seen your eyes before."

"No, but this is the third time I heard that comment, which is making me think I may have some ancestry here. I do not know for sure." Jack shrugged his shoulders and thought about Erd when she first told him he was a descendant of Berbers.

"You will hear that a lot with your eyes and that nose." Salman smiled into the rearview mirror. "Welcome home."

Jack tried to ignore Salman, but Thomas could not resist saying, "Yeah, my Berber brother. You got roots." He laughed and for a moment, the vehicle was full of laughter. Jack tossed two bottled waters to the front seat and said, "Okay. I got it. Now let's find Erd."

The mood turned serious for the rest of the ride up the winding, narrow mountain road. Thomas avoided looking to his left as they climbed in elevation, hoping his fear of heights would not turn his stomach. Finally, Salman turned off the engine and pointed up the mountain where steps had been cut into the stone one hundred feet to the entrance.

Thomas looked up to the top and said, "She could not be up there. It is too remote."

Salman said, "There is only one other site on the mountain, thirty kilometers from here."

"Let's check this one out quickly. We are running out of time," cautioned Thomas as he looked at his watch.

Jack volunteered to go up to look around with Salman, leaving Thomas to stay with the vehicle. Salman led the way up the stairs. As the two men climbed, stones broke away and rolled down the steps to the road.

"Berbers have a rich history in North Africa," said Salman, breathing heavily as he went up the crooked steps.

"Yeah, I know. I have done some reading since I learned of my African ancestors," Jack mumbled from the strain of climbing the steep steps.

Finally at the top, the two men separated to look around for clues of Erd's whereabouts. Jack had the only flashlight. They moved deeper into the mountain's cave. The mosque was built inside an enormous cavern inside the mountain. Salman stopped in the main meditation hall to show Jack a painting on the wall. He said, "Jack, look over to the right with the flashlight."

Jack pointed the light to the area and found a historic battle scene painted on the wall of men dressed like Salman, on horseback with swords and shields drawn. They were near a castle. Salman said, "This is a scene from the battle that gave the Moors dominion over Spain. See the eyes of the Berber horsemen?" he said with pride in his voice.

Jack said, "Impressive."

Salman responded, "Yes, this painting has been here for eight hundred years. Do you feel the history, your history?"

Jack reluctantly agreed. He noticed the resemblance between himself and the men in the painting. *Is this why Erd sent us here?* he thought.

The two men stood in silence, then continued the search until Thomas blew the horn on the vehicle as a signal that it was time to move on.

* * * * *

Twenty feet from the last step, Jack slipped, tumbled, and rolled the rest of the way down the mountainside to the truck. Thomas had fallen asleep while waiting for the two men to return. The loud thud of Jack's body against the Rover door startled Thomas. He reached for his gun and got out of the vehicle to see what happened. Salman was kneeling over Jack when Thomas got there. He poured some water on Jack's face to wake him.

Jack opened his eyes and said, "It's you. I was hoping for ten virgins."

"Brother, it is not your time," responded Salman.

"Old man, get up from there. We have some ground to cover." Thomas reached down to pull Jack up from under the vehicle.

Jack gained his balance and then looked up the mountain to see from where he had fallen. He said, "Ten years ago I would have caught my balance and landed on my feet. I need something stronger than water to clear my head."

Salman handed Jack a leather pouch from his backpack and said, "Drink, drink, you will like. This is Mahia fig brandy, distilled from dates. This will clear your head."

Jack took a sip, coughed, and took a longer drink. "This is good stuff. "

"Good yes?" Salman said, smiling at Jack while he took another drink.

"It's not scotch, but not bad," Jack said with a grin then passed the pouch back to Salman.

Thomas took a sip too. He commented, "I see what you mean. It's a little rough around the edges but it smoothes out after the first sip. Okay, let's get going. We have one more location to check."

Salman started the truck, and the three men continued their journey through the Atlas Mountains. Jack struck up a verse of an Irish drinking song as he took another sip of the Mahia. Bouncing over gravel roads and potholes, the three sang until Jack fell asleep. He woke with a loud scream, "ஆகும் கத்தியை எங்கே"

Thomas asked, "Jack, what did you say?"

"ஆகும் கத்தியை எங்கே", responded Jack.

Salman said, "He is speaking the language of the Moors, Tamil. He said, "Where is the dagger?""

Puzzled Thomas said, "I didn't know Jack could speak that language."

Jack said, "பெயர் என் ?கூறினார் யார் ஜாக் அவர் உள்ளது நடந்தபடி."

"He said who is Jack? My name is Akin," translated Salman.

"He bumped his head when he fell off the mountain," said Thomas.

Jack went back to sleep. Thomas and Salman looked at each other and then drove the next twenty kilometers in silence.

CHAPTER 14

The New Jersey Turnpike hummed with bumper-to-bumper traffic. Dr. Easton agreed to be blindfolded for the final hour of his trip to the laboratory. That little detail was not included in the agreement he had signed earlier. Easton was anxious to get to work. His mind was filled with equations that had haunted him for more than twenty years. The failure to complete his formula for a revolutionary laser design dogged him. He would do anything to solve the puzzle, even if it meant he would not remember anything afterward.

The van turned off the exit, then onto an unmarked two-lane road. Dawson turned Easton's seat around a few times to have him ride backward to skew his orientation if he ever tried to retrace the route to the lab. The paved roadway gave way to gravel on the last mile to the farmhouse. A security gate and an electrified fence guarded the final destination for Dawson and Easton. The van drove into a huge building where an overhead door closed behind them. The driver took Easton's bag with him while Dawson gave his guest the tour of the facility.

The door to the lab required a retina scan to enter. The living quarters were upstairs, overlooking the main floor. It became clear to Dr. Easton that he would not leave the lab until his work was complete. The first stop was at the machine Dawson had partially built from the sketches discovered on the two emeralds and the scrolls found in the handle of the dagger.

The design intrigued Easton. It looked like a sled. Lenses made of quartz were installed in a diagonal formation for light to refract at a downward angle. Two cylinders, a large cylinder with a smaller cylinder inside, made of gold and silver, were spaced directly in line with the quartz beam. Behind the cylinder were three rolls of lithium screens in what looked like a vapor chamber. On the other side of the vapor chamber was the laser lens assembly with a ruby-colored glass.

On the whiteboard next to the machine was the complete formula that Dr. Easton longed to see. He walked around the machine and studied the formula. He inspected the quartz stones located at the point of energy input for the laser. After thirty minutes he said, "What is it?"

Dawson responded, "I'm not sure. The design is similar to a crude laser, but these materials are not compatible with what I know about laser technology. The power source is filtered by quartz stones, which is unusual. However, as you can see in the design schematic, the stones are where they're supposed to be."

"Yes, I see. Who designed this machine?" Dr. Easton asked, looking closely at the quartz stones. "The stones are unusual … they have a glow about them. Why are they so bright? Have they been positively charged?"

"I have to admit, I don't have any answers. The machine's design is from a script found in an ancient dagger recovered recently. The formula for the laser design is from the same source. When we finished building the machine and reworked the formula, I realized this was very similar to the problem I worked on with you as a research assistant. That is why I brought the project to you."

Dr. Easton pointed to the sketch where the lens would be directed. He said, "What is that in front of the device? Is that lead or glass?"

"We are working on this last piece. It is a solid gold panel a quarter of an inch thick. It is to be mounted in front of the laser beam," Dawson said sheepishly, while looking at the floor.

"Did you say a solid gold plate a quarter of an inch thick on a three by three foot sheet? That will cost you a fortune."

"Yes, sir. We are fabricating the plate this evening."

"Incredible. What is this thing?" Easton scratched his head, looking at the design and the stones. "What's your power source?"

"I am not sure. I was planning to use a standard laser, but now I'm not sure. I think we need a natural source," responded Dawson.

"Natural power source?" questioned Easton.

"Yes, sunlight with enhanced ultraviolet properties. We have retrofitted a grain silo with mirrors to create a chamber to direct the light beam through the quartz," responded Dawson, looking at his notes on the whiteboard.

"Interesting work. What do you want me to do?" Easton asked as he started writing notes on the whiteboard.

"Well, for one thing, check my work to be sure I don't blow up New Jersey in the process," Dawson responded, gravely serious.

"Son, don't worry, I won't let you blow us up." Dr. Easton smiled and patted Dawson on his back.

"I am very proud of you. You turned out to be a real scientist. Let me take a few hours to check the formula and crunch a few numbers. I think you are on to something with the natural light. This is a lot to digest. I'm ready to get started." Easton pulled off his jacket and started to work.

Relieved that he had his old professor on board, Dawson walked out to the smelter where his assistant was working on the gold panel. His phone rang. It was Thomas.

"Erd is missing…kidnapped in Egypt. We think they are after the dagger. We only have twenty-four hours to save her. How far along are you?"

Dawson was sweating from the heat from the smelter. He said, "Thomas, we're close. We need more time. I have Dr. Easton reviewing the project. We haven't determined if this thing is a weapon or a tool."

"Erd may be dead, or worse, if she told everything to those who captured her, including the location of the dagger," announced Thomas. "You are running out of time. Increase security at the facility. Get it done!"

The phone went silent. Dawson's hands started to shake. He dropped the phone into the molten gold. His assistant quickly retrieved the phone, but it was ruined. Dawson's hands were still shaking from his conversation with Thomas. He walked out to the main floor in the lab to check on Dr. Easton's progress. Sweat was still rolling down his cheeks and his shirt was soaking wet.

Easton said, "Dawson, you don't look well. Are you all right?"

"Yes, we just finished smelting the gold plate for the machine. It was hot work. The plate should be cool enough in a few hours to handle for installation. Have you made any progress on reviewing my work?" Dawson wiped the sweat from his head with a towel.

"Splendid. We will need the gold plate soon. I made a few corrections to some of the assumptions on the refraction angles and adjusted the quartz lens. The gas vapor chamber is intriguing. This simple design eliminates electronic circuitry. It's pure energy, very powerful. How did they figure this out?" Easton said while cleaning his glasses. "The natural light beam is what this was designed for. However, Light-emitted diode (LED) light may work, too."

* * * * *

A thunderstorm raged outside. Hail pelted the roof of the laboratory while Dawson and Dr. Easton toiled on the ancient machine. The sound of the hail on the metal roof reminded Dawson of the potential danger he faced if Erd was forced to give up the location of the dagger. Simon promised to send extra security, but no one had shown up yet.

"We will have no way to control this thing if we get it to work," said Dr. Easton as he wrestled the gold-plated shield into place on the front of the machine. He continued, "We need to solve this problem before we test."

"To control the power source, we can just shut down the beam," responded Dawson,

"I hope you are right." Dr. Easton inspected the lithium chamber. "If the weather clears we will be ready to test in a few hours."

Dawson completed the last adjustment on the gold shield and then invited Dr. Easton to his office. On his desk was the dagger, separated into pieces from his initial analysis. The scroll was preserved under glass to protect it from air and the elements.

"Is this the source of the design for our project?" asked Dr. Easton

"Yes, it is a one-thousand-year-old, ancient Moor dagger. Striking design, isn't it?" said Dawson.

"Moors, really? Interesting. I received my masters in physics from Oxford. The great universities of Europe, even Oxford, benefited from the Moors' mathematics and science. Why hide this information in a dagger, of all things?" questioned Easton as he inspected the object. He focused on the blade then said, "I think this is platinum. There is more here, Dawson. I believe part of the blade should be incorporated into the machine."

The two men immediately huddled over the scroll and the images encrypted in the emerald stone to confirm Easton's observation.

CHAPTER 15

Military police were waiting for Jamal and Zek to exit their plane when they arrived in Alexandria. Goode had called ahead to clear the way for them to have an official role in the investigation of the death of the plane's crew and the disappearance of Miss Erd. The local authorities granted Zek access to security video footage outside of the hanger where the plane was parked for service. Unfortunately, the cameras had been disabled inside the hanger. The video showed four masked men in maintenance uniforms rolling a large trunk to a cargo plane on the tarmac. The plane was registered as a regional airfreight carrier that serviced Europe and northern Africa. Contact with company officials revealed that the plane had been stolen earlier that day. The bodies of the crew were found in a dumpster behind the hanger. The body count was up to seven. Police and army personnel were everywhere, with automatic weapons, patrolling the area.

The chief of security stopped Jamal outside the surveillance room and asked him questions. "Why did your plane stop in Alexandria for refueling? Does your company have any business in Egypt? This shooting smells of drugs to me," he said, looking at Jamal's face for his reaction.

"Look, we have three dead people and a colleague missing. Search the plane if you want, there is no contraband. We represent a historical society. Do your job!" shouted Jamal, sounding frustrated while pushing the door open to see the video footage.

The security chief followed Jamal into the room. "We may need to ask some more questions. Don't make any plans to leave Alexandria until you talk to me."

Jamal shrugged and sat down next to Zek in front of the computer terminal. Under his breath he said, "I hate pigs and they hate me."

"We have most of what we need. I downloaded the video on the flash drive. Air traffic control tracked the cargo plane to Morocco's airspace, but the plane disappeared from radar. Authorities in Morocco have not reported where the plane landed. Don't worry about the chief. Let me talk to him. His butt is on the line with seven dead bodies and no suspects," responded Zek.

"I guess you're right. He just looked at me like I'm a criminal or something, talking about drugs and stuff. I went off," said Jamal.

"He was trying to push your buttons to get a rise out of you. Police suspect everyone, even you. We are finished here. Let's check out the plane and talk to the investigator in the hanger to see if there are any witnesses," said Zek pulling out the flash drive from the computer.

"I will let you do the talking. I could end up getting us locked up if that security chief charges at me again," responded Jamal.

* * * * *

Morocco where authorities discovered the stolen, burned-out cargo plane on an abandoned airstrip not far from the airport. Police investigators inspected the plane wreckage but found no clues of the kidnappers' identities. Local authorities obtained satellite photographs of the area to determine how the kidnappers were transported from the burned-out plane. The images were not helpful.

Zek arranged transport to the site. Jamal let Zek do all the talking to avoid another situation like they'd had at the Alexandria Airport. On the ground at the burned-out cargo plane, Zek found the cockpit still smoking from the fire. A violent sandstorm had removed any signs of footprints and tire tracks. It was a dead end. Erd was in Morocco, but where was she?

Moroccan authorities left the site. The Atlas Mountains overlooked the wreckage. Jamal and Zek stayed behind, thinking about Erd and looking for any clues that would lead them to her.

Crawling on his hands and knees in the cargo bay, Zek sifted through the charred debris. Jamal walked around the perimeter of the airstrip, looking for tire tracks of the vehicle that carried the terrorists away from the wreckage. Suddenly, sniper bullets whizzed by Jamal's head, forcing him to fall to the ground to find cover. Jamal shouted over to Zek, "We got company. There's a sniper in the hills." Three more shots rang out, chipping away at the boulder where Jamal had taken cover.

"Do not move," yelled Zek. "Do you see where the shots are coming from?"

"Look up to the hills between the trees to the left. I saw a flash of light after the first shot," responded Jamal as he checked the ammunition in his gun. "I'm pinned down. I don't have a shot."

"Stay down! I will try to move to the right to get a better angle," shouted Zek as he crawled through the plane wreckage.

Two more bullets zipped through the plane, missing Zek by inches.

"There are two shooters," yelled Jamal.

Jamal ran to the mountains and tumbled into thick brush surrounded by boulders. Sniper bullets followed him, nipping his shoulder as he rolled over the boulders. Jamal fired three shots, forcing the sniper to change his position. Zek fired, hitting the first sniper. Blood was flowing freely from Jamal's shoulder as he climbed up the hill in pursuit. He found one body, but the other man fled in a jeep. Jamal waved to Zek to signal the danger had passed.

Jamal was leaning over the sniper's body, looking for ID. Zek inspected the rifle. "This a Vintovka Dragonuv SDV, Soviet-era hardware. We are looking for Russians."

"The shooter had no identification, only his mobile phone and a picture under his hat," said Jamal as he searched the sniper's pockets.

"Let me look at your shoulder. You're bleeding," said Zek.

"It's nothing. The bullet went straight through. I've had worse on the streets of Houston," Jamal said with a shrug as he removed his shirt.

"Jamal, we're not in Houston. An infection could set in quickly here if we don't take care of this wound now. Remember, we still don't know who took Erd," responded Zek. He pulled a medical kit out of his backpack.

"You ex-military cats are always prepared. What's in this kit?" said Jamal, looking over his shoulder while Zek treated his wound.

"You're lucky the bullet went through and didn't take off your arm. The Dragonuv rifle is very effective. In Brazil, our special forces unit trained with it. It's a versatile weapon," Zek said as he finished wrapping the bandage.

Jamal put his shirt on and grabbed the sniper's rifle. "We will return the favor with this thing. Luck had nothing to do with it. It just wasn't my time. This phone may lead us to the kidnappers." He handed the phone to Zek. The two men gathered up their gear and climbed down the mountain to the crash site.

The excitement from the sniper attack dissipated. The wound to Jamal's arm started to throb. The bleeding had stopped, but the pain continued. Jamal asked, "Do you have any pain pills in your kit? This arm is starting to wear me out."

"Only aspirin and I don't think that will help. I gave you an antibiotic shot. It should prevent infection. Drink this olive oil, it should help," Zek said, pulling a small bottle from his backpack.

"Olive oil for pain, no way," responded Jamal.

"It's your choice, but the locals use it. It's better than most over-the-counter pain relievers. Look, we're not going to find a drug store out here," Zek said.

"I will try anything to stop the throbbing, but don't come at me with hawk feathers and start chanting stuff," Jamal said with a laugh, and then drank the bottle of olive oil.

Zek sat in the car, studying the mobile phone he'd found on the sniper's body. The phone did not have any numbers programmed in it and had received only one call. Zek called the number. A man answered.

"Hello."

"Who am I speaking to?" asked Zek

"I am the man at the pay phone, who else?" responded the stranger.

"Can you tell me where the pay phone is located?" asked Zek

"Yeah, Newark, New Jersey," the man said and then hung up the phone.

Zek was puzzled by the call. He said to Jamal, "Why would the sniper get a call from Newark?"

"We need to contact Dawson. He's in New Jersey. They may be after him too," shouted Jamal as he reached for his satellite phone. The phone rang but there was no answer. "These guys are all over us. They know too much about our operation. Erd must be talking."

Jamal called Thomas. "We killed a sniper at the crash site. His mobile phone was called from New Jersey. I think they're after Dawson."

"Yeah, I know. I tried to call Dawson too. I warned him that Erd could be giving up information," responded Thomas.

"You think this is similar to what happened to Maalik? Is she dead?" Jamal said as he studied the picture found on the dead sniper.

"No, she is still alive, probably drugged. We have something they want," responded Thomas.

"Yeah, but Dawson is an engineer, not one for this rough stuff," grunted Jamal.

"He will be fine. Keep following the trail on Erd. You are getting closer. Stay on it." Thomas hung up the phone.

Zek drove the car onto the road to follow the direction where the other sniper had fled. The sun was setting. Soon they would need to stop for the night.

CHAPTER 16

The first sign of spring came when ice on the Neva River began to melt. Snow still covered the ground, and the wind howled through the night. Goode noticed more smiles on the faces of strangers he passed in the morning as he walked to what he hoped was the final negotiation session for his first shipment of diamonds to Russia. He thought about Erd, but knew he needed to stay focused.

The purpose of Goode's visit to the Equinox club the night before was to determine if the mafia kidnapped Erd in order to put pressure on his negotiations. But Napoli appeared to be unaware of the plot.

Goode arrived early at the hotel where the negotiations were being held, as was his usual routine. He liked being first. He felt it gave him the advantage in negotiations, though he was thousands of miles away from home.

Napoli was waiting in the lobby. Goode greeted him with a traditional Russian greeting, then said, "Any news on my little problem?"

"When you finish today, come by the club. We can talk better there. I like your diamonds. I think you will be happy with your meeting today," Napoli whispered in his ear and then motioned for his driver to get the car.

Goode waved good-bye and proceeded to the conference room. Napoli was right. The diamond broker arrived with his attorney and banker. Documents were prepared for the bank's line of credit and security details for a series of diamond shipments for a total of twenty thousand carats from the mines controlled by Goode's company. Fatigue had set in by lunchtime when the final documents were signed. Goode decided to forego his usual walk back to his hotel and took a taxi instead. *I need to recharge. There can be no celebration, with Erd missing and feared dead*, thought Goode as he walked past the front desk to the elevator.

He went into his room and then ran the shower to refresh before meeting with Napoli. After his shower, he grabbed his robe from the bed and noticed blood. Under the white bedspread, he discovered the cause of the stain. He found a small finger. It looked like a pinky finger. It could be a woman's.

Erd's finger, he thought.

He searched the bed for a note or anything to tell him what the finger meant or who had sent it, but found nothing. Goode remembered what Napoli had said: the mafia would have sent a body part with the note, not a strand of hair. He thought, *Twenty-four hours has not passed yet. Why cut off her finger? What are their terms for her release?*

Goode placed the finger in a plastic bag and finished dressing. He called Thomas. "I found a finger in my bed a few moments ago. We are running out of time. They should contact me in about eight hours with their terms. I think the Russian mafia may be involved, but I'm not sure which crime family sent the finger. This may be just a sick joke from whoever they are."

"We are tracking Erd's captors from Alexandria but nothing is firm. I will keep you informed," said Thomas before terminating the call.

Thoughts of the small finger in his pocket sent Goode's mind racing. *Did they really cut off Erd's finger? What do they want?* The taxi stopped in front of the Equinox club. The doorman escorted Goode to Napoli's office. He was deep in thought when Napoli entered the room. Goode greeted him and asked if they could talk in private. With the door closed, Goode placed the severed finger on Napoli's desk.

Napoli was surprised, initially, to see the small brown finger. Then he became excited. "This is great news. Now we know who we are dealing with. The finger is a trademark of the Remanche crime family. They like to cut the little ones off first. When did you get this?"

"This morning after the meeting, I found it in my room. There was no note, just a little brown finger in my bed. What does it mean?" said Goode.

"These new gangsters watch too many movies. They want to be like your US godfather. They want drama and blood. This is not good for business, but we must deal with them. They control the liquor and drugs in St. Petersburg. The finger means she is still alive, but we must act quickly. They know you have a relationship with me. This is how they communicate. Do you have anything to trade?"

Goode reached in his pocket for the package he received yesterday. He opened it and poured the contents on the desk. Three diamonds rolled out. Goode said, "This is all I have with me. I have some cash, but as you can see, these are more valuable than cash."

"Yes my friend, they are. This morning I found out more about the woman that delivered the note to you yesterday. That is why I asked you to meet me. But now that you have the finger, I know who is behind your trouble here."

"What do we do?" asked Goode as he picked up the diamonds and put them back in the box.

Napoli dialed his mobile phone then shouted in Russian. Later in a calmer voice, he finished his conversation. He said to Goode, "I set up a meeting for one hour from now. The Remanche knew you were under my protection yet they do this. I hate this business. There is no honor." Napoli pounded the table and ordered a bottle of vodka.

He said, "We drink now." He placed his .45 automatic on his desk and poured two glasses half full. "To friends and dead strangers, yes?"

Napoli raised his glass and looked into Goode's eyes. His cold blue eyes peered through Goode. Goode thought, *Am I the friend or the stranger*, as he drank down the vodka. Napoli poured another drink and ordered his assistant to have the car brought to the rear.

CHAPTER 17

The darkness gave way to light halfway up the mountain. An ancient mosque, carved into the stone, sat majestically on the side of the mountain. The University of Marrakesh had converted the thousand-year-old structure into a record archive. A barricade marked the closed road. The checkpoint was unmanned. Salman jumped out of the vehicle to raise the barricade arm and let the Rover through. Jack was still asleep. Thomas decided to let him sleep, as he thought Jack's head injury from the fall was more serious than he'd thought. The truck came to a stop at the bottom of the stairs at the entrance of the once great mosque. Salman thought it was closed. But to his surprise, the lights were on.

Thomas and Salman gathered their backpacks to go inside. Thomas held his gun in one hand, and Salman led the way.

Jack shouted, "Hey, hey wait for me," as he ran to catch up. "You guys are not going to leave me out of the action." He had his 9mm in hand as he followed behind Thomas.

Thomas said, "Who's going to watch the truck?"

"Nobody wants that relic. Trust me, it's not going anywhere," Jack said with a grin.

Salman pushed the huge door. Slowly, the door opened, making a loud creaking sound.

"Well, so much for surprise," said Thomas as they walked into the enormous hall. The light they had seen from the road was coming from a room off the huge hall. Jack led the way, crouching low with his gun drawn. Salman and Thomas followed closely behind him.

The door opened up to a small chapel with an enclave for an office. The light source was from candles in the front of the room. After a quick check, Jack waved for Thomas and Salman to enter the room. The three men split up to search but found no one. Finally, they sat down on the bench near the rear of the room.

"Another dead end," said Thomas. He put the revolver back in his waistband. At that moment, they heard the big door at the entrance close with a loud bang. Jack jumped and ran down the hall, leaving Thomas and Salman on the bench. When Jack got to the door, there was no one there.

As Jack walked back to the chapel to report what he'd found, he heard footsteps approaching in the hall. The echo of the footsteps as they slowly approached the room was ominous. The men sat motionless, with guns drawn, as the door opened. Through the door walked a tall dark-skinned man in a silk robe who said, "Peace be upon you."

Only Salman responded, "Peace be with you." He extended his hand. The men shook hands and then gave each other two light cheek-to-cheek kisses, alternating sides. Thomas and Jack quickly put their guns away while watching the exchange of greetings between Salman and the stranger.

The man introduced himself. "I am Rashe, the caretaker of this mosque. I think you know this place is not open to the public. Why are you here at this late hour?" He walked over to Jack to take a closer look at his face.

Salman started to explain. Rashe raised his hand and said, "Enough. Who is this one?" He pointed to Jack.

"My name is Akin," said Jack.

Salman said, "Who is Akin?"

Jack turned to Thomas and then passed out on the floor. Rashe pointed to the tabletop. Thomas and Salman lifted Jack onto the table while Rashe went for water. Thomas propped Jack's head up with his backpack then fanned him. Sweat rolled down Jack's forehead. They raised his head to help him drink some water and placed a wet compress on his forehead.

"I recognized him from my reading," said Rashe. "That is why I asked about him. His likeness is in the manuscript writing from ancient Moorish Spain." He walked over to his desk to a huge leather-bound book to find the page. Thomas and Salman gathered around the old book that contained handwritten pages and original illustrations. Rashe pointed to the picture of a battle scene with Moorish horsemen. Rashe said, "See the one on the white horse? See his eyes and nose? Oh yes, there is the dagger under his sash."

"Who is that? He does look like Jack," responded Thomas as he examined the picture.

"His name is Akin. He was a hero of this battle in 756 AD. Why did you come here?" responded Rashe.

"A dagger was recovered a few months ago that looks similar to the one on Akin's belt. We have a colleague who has been kidnapped. We believe the kidnappers want the dagger," responded Thomas.

"You are the second group of foreigners to come seeking information on a dagger. Three days ago, four men came to research the archives in search of information concerning a dagger crafted in Moorish Spain. They called it the king's dagger. The dagger has been lost since the defeat of the Moor in 1492 and the fall of Granada. The king had it made for his prime minister," responded Rashe as he looked through the book for a picture of the dagger. He found the dagger in another book to show to Thomas.

"Amazing. This looks similar to our dagger," said Thomas.

"The prime minister was a patron of the sciences for the Moor University in Toledo, Spain. He was an amateur scientist. His specialty was optics. Did you know there were seventeen universities in Moorish Spain, while at the same time in Christian Europe there were only two?"

"No, I did not know that," responded Thomas as he paced the floor.

"Yes, the Moors had over seventy public libraries in the tenth and eleventh centuries, while there were none in Europe."

"The Moors' intellectual achievements are fascinating," commented Thomas while looking at the books on Rashe's desk.

"The men who came three days ago were rude and smelled of Spanish wine. One of them was Russian. I asked them to leave. Later, we discovered one of our priceless books was missing. We notified the police," said Rashe.

Jack rose up to sit on the side of the table. He scratched his head and said, "What's going on?"

Thomas responded, "You passed out a few minutes ago. You were speaking in Tamil, a language used by the Moors. You said your name is Akin."

"What? I can only speak English, and a little Portuguese. Who is Akin? What's going on? Is this from that Moroccan spirit water you gave me?" Jack said, looking at Salman.

"Jack, this is something else. We all drank the Mahia, but you are the only one acting strange. You fell and hit your head, remember?" said Thomas.

"No, I don't remember hitting my head. What's going on?" Jack felt a bruise on the back of his head.

"You may have a concussion, which would explain your memory loss. You should lie down for a while," cautioned Rashe.

CHAPTER 18

The window let in sunlight that warmed Erd's face. The sweatshirt covered her arms but left her bronze thighs exposed. The bed made her feel more secure. The warmth of the sheets helped her mind to relax. Erd dreamed about Thomas lying next to her. She felt his hands on her breasts, stroking her thighs, making her want him more. She started to moan. Her thighs shivered with the thought of Thomas inside her. His body was heavy on her chest. His breath was hot on her neck. He whispered in her ear. She called out Thomas's name.

It was not Thomas. Stark had slipped into her room. He straddled her body, pulling up her blindfold so she could see his chiseled face and disfigured nose. Erd screamed in terror. She cried out as loud as she could. She faded in a daze, muttering between consciousness and a dream state. The drugs were working.

Two hours had passed since the last questioning session. The guard loaded her on the cart and strapped her into the chair. The drip of green fluid into her arm continued. The doctor entered the room to check her vital signs. She asked a few questions to see if the drug was working as planned.

Erd screamed, "Why don't you just kill me. I am already dead." She cried and sobbed uncontrollably until the doctor injected her arm with more drugs.

The doctor waited a few minutes then asked the questions again. Erd responded robotically, answering every question without pause. The recorder captured every word. A few hours later, the doctor noticed blood on Erd's legs and examined the cause of the bleeding.

The doctor cleaned up her patient and sent Erd back to her room. She didn't say anything about what she'd found, but she was disturbed that her patient had been sexually assaulted while under her care. Ten years ago, she lost her license to practice medicine due to drug use. Illegal mind control experiments discovered at a mental institute in London resulted in the doctor's permanent ban from medicine in the United Kingdom. She served three years in prison, but still considered herself a doctor.

As a child, the doctor had been raped repeatedly by her uncle until she stabbed him to death. She was a minor; the crime was determined to be self-defense, and her record was expunged. She got counseling until she turned eighteen and then studied to become a doctor. The counseling did not help her deal with the memory of the rape, and murder of her uncle. The drugs helped until she could no longer function at the hospital. Stark found her for his project.

Seeing the blood on Erd's legs triggered memories from the time when the doctor was a child. She kept thinking of her uncle coming for her every night until she cut his throat. She woke up the next morning covered with blood and found her dead uncle's body on the floor. She went down for breakfast as if nothing had happened, except there was still blood on her nightgown. Her mother went to her room and discovered her brother's body. She knew immediately what had happened.

The doctor became frantic. She went to the roof for air. Thoughts from her childhood kept flashing in her mind when she thought about Erd being raped in the room next door.

Stark found the doctor on the roof, looking out to the ocean. He said, "When can I move her? We cannot stay here much longer."

"She is responding well to the drugs. I gave her the last injection a few hours ago. The IV treatment should continue for four more hours and then the process should be complete. I noticed that she had been sexually assaulted. Any emotional distress will cause a relapse, and the drug treatment will need to be increased. These are dangerous drugs. They could kill her." The doctor cautioned Stark, hoping the assaults would stop if Stark knew they would hurt the treatment.

"Look, she means nothing to me. I will do what I like. Just give her more drugs. That's what I pay you to do, right?" Stark pressed his shoulder against the doctor's breasts until she had to move away from him.

The emotions from her childhood rushed over her. The doctor went to the bathroom to splash water on her face. In the mirror, she could see her uncle standing behind her, waiting to take her to bed. Her mind flashed back to taking the knife from the kitchen and then waiting for her uncle to come for her. She replayed in her mind the images of slashing her uncle's throat while she stared into the mirror. The doctor laughed nervously then turned off the light.

The doctor walked into the room and saw that Erd's hands were bound to the bed and her legs tied to the rails. Seeing Erd, the doctor saw herself as a young girl. She thought, *I am a doctor. I must protect my patient.* The doctor went to her room and injected herself with morphine. In the mirror, she saw her uncle standing behind her again. She said, "No. You will not get her, too! I will stop you!"

Frantic, the doctor ran to Erd's room. She sent the guard away. The doctor used smelling salts to wake Erd and put her on a cart. She rolled Erd to the laundry room and then rolled her onto the floor.

"You must run! I will give you something to help you." The doctor injected Erd with adrenaline.

Erd jumped. Suddenly alert, she said, "Where am I?"

"No time for that, put these clothes on now," urged the doctor.

Erd put on the oversized clothes. She said, "I know your voice. Why are you helping me?"

"There is no time. You need to slide down the laundry chute and get out of here now!" The doctor pushed Erd toward the cabinet and helped her into the chute. "Go, go now!"

Erd heard pounding on the door as she slid down the chute. Frightened, she turned her mind to Thomas, hoping he could receive her thoughts before her captors caught her.

In the basement, Erd's heart thumped loudly from the adrenaline shot. She felt like it would burst. Not knowing where to go, she opened the door and ran up the stairs.

Erd could see nothing but the ocean. Waves crashed on the wall below. The mist splashed on her face, and for a brief moment, she felt alive again. Erd looked up at the beacon on the lighthouse tower. From behind her, a guard grabbed her and stuck a stun gun to her neck.

A nude body, without teeth and fingertips was found hours later on the beach. Stark no longer needed the doctor.

CHAPTER 19

Sunsets on the frozen Neva River in St. Petersburg were memorable. An aging gray Mercedes sedan sped past the riverfront where barges lined the port, waiting for the ice to break. Goode's thoughts were not on sunsets. The driver smoked a foul-smelling cigarette that made the ride even more nerve racking. Napoli pulled out his .45 automatic. He removed the clip then handed the gun to Goode. "This was my father's gun. He fought the Germans in two wars. See the pearl handle. Stalin himself gave him this gun after the siege in Stalingrad. Feel the grip. Be careful, it has a hair trigger."

"It is a fine weapon," responded Goode as he handed the gun back to Napoli. "Are we expecting trouble?"

"This is Russia. We sometimes disagree. I always expect trouble." Napoli smiled as he looked at his gun.

The skyline faded behind them as the car came to a stop at an abandoned warehouse near the port. Napoli's men followed in a car behind them. His men went in first. Goode followed with Napoli. Inside, two men were seated around the table. A bottle of vodka sat at the center of the table with shot glasses on a tray nearby.

The host said, "We drink now," as he poured a drink for Napoli and Goode.

"No drink." Napoli asked Goode for the severed finger and tossed it on the table. He said, "You disrespect me and my guest with this. Why you do this?" Napoli's cold blue eyes stared directly at his host.

Tension suddenly rose to a boiling point. Guns became visible around the conference table as the men waited for the silence to break with the host's response.

"I am a business man. This little finger is an invitation for a meeting. You are here. I am here. Let's talk business. We require a little knife in return for the rest of the body that belongs to this finger. It is a dagger. I think it is called," the man said as he poured his glass of vodka and drank it.

"This man is under my protection. You dishonor me with this." Napoli responded by pulling out his gun and firing once at the man sitting next to his host. The man's body slumped over the table then rolled onto the floor. "Now I drink," responded Napoli. He poured himself a drink while holding his gun on his host.

"Good, now we talk business," said the host nervously while his men took out the body.

"Is this body alive that belongs to the finger?" Napoli responded. He poured Goode a glass of vodka and urged him to drink up.

"Yes, she is no value dead, right?" the host responded then poured more vodka.

"I require proof of life before we can consider your demand," said Napoli as he poured another drink.

"You will have it. When can we have the dagger?" asked the host.

"Is there anything you will accept instead?" responded Napoli.

The man tossed over another finger then said, "No, only the dagger. In eight hours or the woman lives no longer."

Goode was shocked to see the other finger thrown so casually on the table. He attempted to stand and reach across the table to grab the host, but Napoli's men restrained him.

Napoli stood up to leave. "Understood. Send the proof of life. You understand if any other body parts are removed, the deal is off." Napoli put his gun back in his waistband and walked out. In the car, he said, "Good meeting. This is a dirty business. Can you produce this dagger? These people have little honor. They will kill the woman in eight hours. There is nothing I can do."

"I understand. I will work on getting the dagger. Why did you shoot the man at the table?" Goode inquired as he wiped sweat from his temple in an attempt to stay calm.

"I never liked him. This was as good a time as any to let him know. We have an old saying 'My enemy's enemy is my friend,'" responded Napoli while pouring a glass of vodka. "No worries. You are under my protection. They will not risk a war over this kidnapping. This is just business."

The driver stopped at Goode's hotel. The two men parted, agreeing to meet again when the proof of life was available. Goode tipped his hat at Napoli and walked into the hotel.

When Goode called Thomas, he quickly answered his phone. "The Russians claim to have Erd. They will only trade Erd for the dagger. They produced another finger to make the point that they will kill her. We should have proof of life in a few hours. She has only eight hours to live if we don't produce the dagger," said Goode as he paced the floor in his room.

"Stall as much as you can. We're working it from this end. I will arrange to have the dagger delivered to you soon," Thomas responded.

"These Russians are cold blooded killers," said Goode, looking at the two small brown fingers in the plastic bag on the table.

"I got the picture. Stay focused. We will get her back," Thomas terminated the call to avoid getting emotional.

CHAPTER 20

Blue sky broke through the clouds in New Jersey. The noon sun beamed light directly overhead, into the grain silo at the dairy farm. An electric motor opened up the roof to reveal mirrors to beam the sunlight required for Dawson's laser. The temperature in the silo exceeded 150 degrees, with mirrors directing light to the channel leading to the quartz intake lens.

Dr. Easton handed Dawson safety glasses in preparation for opening the small door to let the sun's rays power the laser. Dawson's heart rate increased with anticipation as he thought about the unknown. The light entered the quartz lens, causing an extremely bright reaction. The reaction created superheated gases in the chamber. The red lens glowed, creating a thin beam focused on the gold plate. Vapors from the chamber produced a distortion field around the device, causing the machine to overheat. Dr. Easton pressed the button that closed the silo cover to cut the power, and the gold plate vanished, leaving only the brackets. "Amazing! Where did the gold plate go? Three pounds of gold vanished," said Dawson.

"I don't know. It was here one minute and gone the next," responded Dr. Easton.

Standing where the gold plate had been installed, the two men studied the machine. A loud bang could be heard from outside the garage doors of the lab. Dawson first thought intruders were coming for the dagger. His assistant came from the area where they'd heard the sound. He said, "Sir, you need to come outside to see this."

Dawson and Easton followed the man through the garage and watched the door move up slowly. The van was parked in the driveway. The assistant pointed to the roof of the van where the gold plate was lodged in the roof behind the driver's seat.

"How did this happen? It's like the gold plate was teleported into the van. Impossible," said Dr. Easton.

Dawson opened the door to the van to inspect the gold plate. "It's fused into the metal of the van. The plate traveled one hundred feet through the lab roof, and into the van," responded Dawson as he ran back to the lab to determine if the object had been propelled through the roof, but he found no signs of damage.

"Did the machine create a wormhole to transport the plate into the van or did the plate dematerialize to move this distance? How did it become fused with the van? The plate is in the same form as it was before we turned on the machine," said Dr. Easton as he examined the gold plate in the van's roof.

"Are you crazy? You can't be serious. A wormhole is a passage through space-time. It's impossible; this must be something else. We must know what really happened," responded Dawson. He paced while examining the damage to the van.

"Let's do it again. We should review the video." Dr. Easton spoke with nervous excitement. He held a hammer and chisel in his hand as he wrestled the gold plate from the van's roof.

* * * * *

A commuter flight from Maine landed at Newark Liberty International Airport. The fight was booked as a charter with seven passengers for a plane that could carry thirty. The small airline did not mind. It got a premium for those flights. The cargo bay was reserved for drilling equipment as a part of the charter. Special security arrangements were made to ease US Custom's requirements for the equipment. The men and the equipment were cleared through customs at a hanger facility near the terminal.

Two black sport utility vehicles were parked outside, waiting for the new arrivals. The leader of the group had GPS coordinates for his destination. Safely outside of the airport, the vehicles drove to an abandoned car wash to unpack the boxes shipped with them on the plane. The men easily assembled the assortment of parts into automatic weapons. The Uzi was the weapon of choice for the mission. The 9mm compact submachine gun was easy to conceal in the shipping crates.

The target was a farmhouse fifty miles away near the sleepy town of Vernon. The leader of the group reviewed the mission profile on his phone, while the rest of his crew donned black uniforms and painted their faces. Miss Erd had given Stark the frequency and the codes for the GPS tracking device inserted in the carrying case for the dagger. She had also given him a detailed description of the dagger during one of Stark's many interrogation sessions. Stark had everything he needed.

The kidnapping note and severed fingers provided to Goode in St. Petersburg had been a diversion. Stark and his Russian partner never intended to trade Erd for the dagger, but he needed to keep her alive until he had the object in his possession. His partner in the Russian mafia had acted to throw the African Brotherhood off Erd's trail. It was working.

CHAPTER 21

Jack was awake again. He remembered speaking in a strange language. Strangely enough, now he understood what he was saying. His head was throbbing. Standing over him was Thomas, Rashe, and Salman. They had moved him below the main floor to the living quarters. His room was a large suite with stone columns. The windows looked out to a courtyard facing the valley. Steel bars guarded the room from the outside.

"Jack, do you remember me?" said Thomas

"Yeah, you block head, I remember everything. You got me into this mess in the first place," said Jack as he rubbed the knot on the back of his head.

"Great, you sound more like the old Jack," responded Thomas.

"Can anyone tell me what's going on? Who is this Akin I heard about before I passed out?" Jack held ice on his head.

"You do resemble him. I am Rashe, the caretaker of this place. Akin is what we call him, but no one really knows who he is. His likeness appears in historical works of art dating back to the eighth century. Artists have painted his likeness in battle scenes and courts of the various kings of Moorish Spain and in Marrakesh. Since you've been in Morocco, several persons have recognized your face, right?"

"Well, yeah, but that does not mean anything," said Jack rubbing his eyes.

"Akin is a heroic figure in the writings as well. Before you arrived last night, I was reading an account in the great book about a mysterious stranger who saved the day at the battle of Musara. Before the king could honor him, he vanished, and from a description from those fighting that day, the artist compiled this picture." Rashe held up the oversized leather-bound book and turned to the page to show Jack the picture.

"Get out of town!" Jack screamed. "That is not me."

"I know, but you cannot deny the likeness is very close to yours," responded Rashe. "You asked for your dagger last night. Look at the dagger under his sash in the painting."

"Yeah but who is this guy?" asked Jack

"No one knows. He disappeared until one hundred years later," Rashe said, picking up another huge book and turning several pages. "See this man standing behind the Moor King of Toledo? The last time his image was recorded was in Granada in the fifteenth century."

"Yes, he looks like the other guy," responded Jack

"He looks like you, too. I'll be happy to show you many more books and paintings where this man whom we call Akin shows up over a period of six centuries. He is a mysterious figure. All the artists and authors are different, but his likeness is the same. There is a legend of a spirit that lingers and will not die. This Akin embodies this spirit even to this day. They say he takes over the body of a willing host."

Salman said, "Yes, at the first mosque we visited last night, we saw him on a white horse in a painting of a battle scene."

"Don't look at me like that. I remember the painting. I fell down the stairs afterward," said Jack.

"The dagger is significant. He is always shown with the dagger," responded Rashe.

"I did help Erd locate the dagger in Great Zimbabwe," said Jack as he stood to walk to the window. "Why did Erd send us here?"

"The key may be in the book stolen by the men who came a few days ago. Maybe she read their minds and saw the book and this place. Rashe, what was contained in the book?" asked Thomas.

"It was a book of science with translated text from the Greeks and Egyptians. It was very detailed on optics. It had writing in the margins. I think it is from the thirteenth century, based on the book bindings," said Rashe as he looked through an index of the archived documents. He continued, "We recently discovered a series of manuscripts in the cellar that described something the Moors were developing. By the thirteenth century, gunpowder and cannons were used to defend castles in Seville. An arms race of sorts in the Middle Ages began to perfect the use of gunpowder to gain the advantage in battle. Soon it was feared that knights and heavy armor would become obsolete. A Moorish scientist discovered a unique stone recovered from a meteorite that struck a hillside outside Seville. The stone glowed in sunlight. It had special properties. Soon experiments with the new stone revealed they could create a bright light beam when directed toward sunlight that could temporarily blind opposing forces on the battle field."

"Is this the information in the book stolen a few days ago?" asked Thomas.

"Yes, they only got one of the three books; the other two were in Marrakesh being refurbished. We received them this morning," responded Rashe.

"Do you mind if I take a look at the remaining two books?" asked Thomas.

"No, they're underground in the vault. You cannot see the actual books, but we had all of them scanned at the university. I can pull up the images on the computer." Rashe directed Thomas to follow him to his office.

Gathered around the computer at Rashe's desk, the three men waited while the computer warmed up. The screen blinked and, finally, Rashe could bring up the images from the stolen book.

In disbelief, Thomas looked at Jack and said, "Do you see what I see? This is incredible. That looks like a crude laser. How is this possible?"

"It's impossible," agreed Jack.

"These books were discovered only two years ago, hidden in a crypt in Marrakesh, lost for over seven hundred years," said Rashe.

"Did you see the dagger?" said Thomas.

"Yeah, that's our little knife," responded Jack.

"They must have discovered the secret of the dagger. Shortly after stealing this book, they captured Erd," said Thomas. "The dagger is not safe."

Thomas left the room to use the satellite phone to contact Dawson to warn him. He got no answer.

* * * * *

Dawson's nerves were getting the best of him. He couldn't hold the secret from his friend Dr. Easton any longer. Walking back to the lab, Dawson said, "I would like to do this experiment again, but I am afraid it's not safe here. This machine is powerful. We still don't know what it is, but there are others after the dagger I showed you in my office."

"We must continue; we are so close," said Easton

"These are dangerous people. They will kill to get the dagger and our research," said Dawson as he closed the door behind him.

"You have security here," said Easton.

Dawson responded, "Not enough. We are isolated out here on the farm."

"Look, we have much more work to do. Let's use my lab. Whoever these people are, they do not know me. Besides, my lab is Department of Defense certified. They would have to break in through the army's security to get to the dagger," said Dr. Easton, holding the solid gold plate in his hand.

"You know we cannot share this discovery with anyone. Remember the nondisclosure agreement you signed," said Dawson as he walked past the machine.

"Don't worry. I didn't want to tell you…but I have cancer. It's terminal. That's really why I agreed to do this super-secret project. I've only got three months left. Your secret is safe with me, son. This project has been my life's work."

Dawson was stunned by Dr. Easton's announcement. He said, "Why didn't you tell me? I would not have involved you with all of this had I known. Are you sure about the diagnosis? You need to be with your family."

"We never had any children. My wife, Judy, passed away five years ago. All I have is my work now." Tears fell from Dr. Easton's eyes as he thought about his wife of thirty years.

"I can't let you do this," said Dawson with his hands over his eyes.

Dr. Easton interrupted Dawson. "You are giving me a chance to make it happen before I die. I just want to see this through. Let me help you," pleaded Dr. Easton. He continued, "It's spring break, there is nobody on campus. We can slip in the back gate, with the van and the machine unnoticed."

The two men stood silently for a few minutes then, reluctantly, Dawson said, fighting back tears, "Okay Doc, if it means that much to you. Let's do this together!" The two men packed the machine in a large trunk and placed the dagger case in Dawson's messenger bag. Quietly, they drove out on the dirt road through a neighboring farm. Dawson told no one he was leaving or where he was going.

Two hours into the drive to Cambridge, a radio newscaster reported on a gunfight at a dairy farm in Vernon, New Jersey. The FBI was called to help the local sheriff with the crime scene. Three bodies were found at the site.

Dawson turned off the radio after hearing the report and said, "We have a two-hour lead on them."

"Speed up. We need to get off the highway. They may have your license plate. Take the next exit and turn off the GPS. Let's find another vehicle. This van is not safe anymore," said Dr. Easton anxiously as he looked out the side-view mirror. "There's a train station three miles away. I suggest we take the train the rest of the way."

Dawson exited the freeway.

The train station was deserted, except for a few taxis waiting outside the building. The next train was not scheduled for another ninety minutes. Dawson felt exposed while waiting in the parking lot with the machine and the dagger. Dr. Easton sat with the tablet computer from the lab, analyzing the video from the last experiment.

"We need to move. Waiting for the train is costing us time." Dawson got out of the van and approached a taxi driver parked a few cars over.

"Our vehicle overheated. We need to be in Cambridge for a meeting. Do you go that far?" Dawson questioned the driver.

"No, sir, that is an hour away. It will be expensive for you. It will cost you."

"Money is no problem. We really need to make this meeting," insisted Dawson.

"The train would be cheaper, but it's your money. Let's go," said the driver as he turned on his meter, preparing for the drive to Cambridge.

Dawson and Easton loaded the trunk into the taxi. The dagger case fell out of Dawson's bag, breaking the back seal. Dr. Easton discovered a GPS tracking sensor hidden inside the case. He said, "We have trouble. They can track us with this sensor if they have the code. They may be on the way here right now."

Dawson crushed the sensor with the heel of his shoe then checked the van for any other signs that would give away where they were going.

CHAPTER 22

The computer screen beeped for two seconds. Then on the screen, the target area displayed a wave similar to the ripples made by a pebble tossed into a pond, except that the pond was the satellite image of the US Eastern Seaboard. The NASA Jet Propulsion Laboratory (JPL) commissioned a special project to study anomalies in satellite images of the earth's surface. The project had been scheduled to be terminated in a few weeks, until the screen beeped. The technician zoomed in on the area affected by the wave pulse and found that it originated in Vernon, New Jersey.

A scientist named Dr. Shaun McLeay was the JPL project manager. He was asleep in the conference room when the call came from the monitoring station.

"What is this thing? The seismic wave in New Jersey?" his boss asked. He had received a call from the National Security Agency (NSA). He continued, "The FBI is on the ground at a dairy farm that has been converted into a laboratory. There are three dead bodies there. The FBI wants to know if a terrorist action caused the seismic wave."

"Sir, I don't know what would cause the anomaly. The clock on the satellite image is off by four seconds. I've never seen this happen before. It is as if time stopped for a moment." Dr. McLeay rubbed his eyes then read a printout from the event.

"You better get some answers soon. Your office is going to be crawling with agents from the NSA and FBI within the next hour." The phone went silent.

Dr. McLeay called a meeting with his team to review the satellite feed and seismic information to determine what had happened. His colleague, Kaiya Nelson, spoke up. "Sir, this may be a wormhole. I know this sounds strange, but it was not an earthquake or weather event. It's as if the rules of physical science changed for a moment. A wormhole could have caused this." Kaiya was only thirty-one years old. She was the youngest to receive a PhD in her field of quantum mechanics at MIT. She was on the fast track within the agency to become a department head in a few years.

"Are you saying someone in a makeshift lab in a dairy farm opened a wormhole, something we have not been able to do with a billion-dollar budget? Really, do you expect me to believe this?" Dr. McLeay pounded the table, spilling his coffee on the computer printout.

"Sir, we checked our equipment and confirmed the findings with our counterparts in Australia and India. There is no other explanation," responded the young Asian woman wearing black rimmed glasses.

"No, you get on the plane. Go to the site in New Jersey and get me some answers. I cannot believe this. There must be another explanation." Dr. McLeay left the meeting room to greet the first wave of federal agents who were waiting in the lobby. Soon his office would be full of people asking questions. He had no answers but the unbelievable.

Kaiya rushed into her office to gather testing equipment and her backpack from the back of the door and then ran out to a waiting helicopter for the flight to New Jersey. The smell of vanilla followed her. Kaiya used vanilla extract as her perfume of choice, to remind her of her grandmother, who always smelled like cookies. She'd learned her grandma's secret and adopted the fragrance. Besides, it was practical and inexpensive. As a scientist, she could allow this little frill for herself. Her family emigrated from Vietnam and money was always tight. Growing up with five brothers, she never discovered her feminine self. She wore tight-fitting, faded blue jeans with holes in the legs. Her body suited jeans well. Often followed around the office by young interns, she ignored the extra attention, thinking it was her sweet perfume that caught the unwanted attention. However, the former tomboy was actually a striking beauty, hidden behind her black rimmed glasses, baggie shirts, and jeans.

Several other scientists were also on the way to the site. Kaiya would be the team leader until her boss arrived after a briefing at the Pentagon. Her gut told her the event was a wormhole, but she knew it was impossible too.

* * * * *

White tape marked the outline where three bodies were found at the farmhouse in New Jersey. The FBI set up a makeshift command center in the garage, leaving the laboratory untouched until the scientist from NASA inspected the site. Homeland Security monitored the situation with personnel on the ground. The FBI agent in command suspected several bodies had been removed from the crime scene based on the blood pools and the positions of the ones left behind.

He called the field office. "We have too much blood for the bodies found on-site. Whoever started this fight got a bloody nose. The bullets used by the perpetrators are Israeli... for automatic weapons... most likely Uzi. We tracked the two vehicles used in the farmhouse attack to a nearby town. The vehicles were abandoned. A van was reported stolen an hour ago. We suspect they are headed to Boston."

Kaiya and the JPL project team walked by as the agent was making his report. She turned to look at him. He motioned for her to keep walking and pointed to the lab. It was Kaiya's first field assignment to research an anomaly. The blood, police, and guns made it difficult for her to focus. Once inside the lab, she assigned her team to search the area, take pictures of the equipment, check for radiation, and review papers left behind. Whoever had been there had erased the whiteboard and collected all of their notes from the earlier experiment. Nothing helpful was found, except a smelter pot of molten gold and the mirrors installed in the grain silo.

The FBI suspected money laundering and drug trafficking when they found the gold. They estimated twenty-thousand dollars' worth of gold was still in the smelter pot. No signs of drugs made the lab's purpose a mystery. The seismic wave question was why Kaiya was sent to investigate. Her phone rang every fifteen minutes, with her boss asking for an update. Finally, she told Dr.

McLeay, "If you stop calling me, I can get some work done."

"I need some answers. These folks from the Pentagon are breathing down my throat," Dr. McLeay said, frustrated from the pressure.

"I know, but I need some time to analyze the situation. There is nothing here that could cause a seismic wave… only molten gold and a converted grain silo with mirrors. The silo looks like a tunnel designed to intensify sunrays for electromagnetic energy. It appears the sunlight was directed to a specific point, but something is missing. There was something on the table next to the light receptacle that has been removed. That is all I know. I will call you in thirty minutes," responded Kaiya.

Relieved to have more information, he said, "Okay, thirty minutes, not a second longer." He terminated the call.

Kaiya reached into her backpack for an experimental electronic device she had developed as a part of her PhD thesis. The device was designed to measure electromagnetic waves, theoretically, to detect wormholes. Walking around the lab, she measured little or no activity. Ready to give up, she put the device in her backpack. Then a loud buzzing erupted. She was standing where, hours earlier, the gold plate had been installed on the machine. Moments later, she vanished and then reappeared on the ground outside the garage of the farmhouse. Lying on the concrete, she woke up to find FBI agents standing over her. She could not speak immediately, but finally said, "I must have slipped and fallen. I'm okay." She didn't want to disclose what had just happened to her.

The agent in command said, "How did you get out here?"

"Oh, I walked around back and went out the other door by the gold smelter. Really, I am okay."

The FBI agent looked at her as if she were withholding information. He said, "You know we are on the same team. If you find anything, you are required to share that information." He walked back into the garage and whispered something to another agent.

As a scientist, Kaiya knew what had just happened was physically impossible. It defied proven science. Yes, there were theories, but nothing really like what had happened to her. She thought, *How did this happen? Was it my electromagnetic detector or something else?*

Her phone rang. "It's been thirty-five minutes. You are late. What do you have to report?"

"I had a high electromagnetic wave reading. I need to investigate further. Give me an hour to check the calibration of the machine," responded Kaiya as she brushed the dirt from her pants on her way back to the lab.

"No, thirty minutes. That's the deal. Don't be late." Dr. McLeay terminated the call.

Kaiya forgot about national security and her mission as the project leader. She focused on science and discovering the first wormhole. She thought, *This could mean time travel or teleportation. I must be sure.* Kaiya went back to the spot where she'd vanished before. This time she had the wavelength detector in her hand and her camera phone out to record the event. The detector vibrated as before, but this time the experience was different. She did not pass out. Instead, she watched herself dissolve in a vacuum and then in an instant she was gone.

Thirty minutes later, Dr. McLeay called her phone but got no answer. He contacted her project team members, but no one knew where she was. A search was initiated but there was no sign of her two hours later. The FBI opened a new investigation. They ordered everyone out of the lab.

* * * * *

Erd's few moments of freedom unleashed her mind enough to scream for help. Her thoughts reached far away, to New Jersey, to warn Dawson, but instead, in a moment of synchronicity, Erd had channeled her mental energy to the lab while Kaiya was making the second test of the wormhole. Kaiya woke to the sound of the ocean, where Erd had been recaptured under the lighthouse tower. She startled the guard. He immediately tied her up and took her to Stark.

"Who are you?" asked Stark

"Kaiya Nelson," she responded, confused by the new environment and the guns pointing at her. She assumed the men were responsible for the dead bodies in the farmhouse.

"Where did you come from?" he asked

Kaiya did not answer. She stopped talking, knowing that everything she said could put her in more danger.

"Oh, you're holding your words, too." Stark slapped her face then ordered his men to lock her up with the other one.

With the doctor dead, he thought the drugs might not be effective. Stark was running out of time. Kaiya was tied to a chair in the room with Erd, who was strapped to the bed. Erd was unconscious, with an IV drip in her arm. Kaiya closed her eyes, hoping she would wake up from the nightmare, but the blood dripping from her nose onto her pants brought the reality of the situation into focus. Her quest for science was replaced with intense fear. Terrorists with a device that could create wormholes for teleportation could cause international chaos. Kaiya suspected her host did not know about the wormhole, but she knew, if tortured, she would talk.

Looking at Erd, Kaiya said, "Did you do this? Did you bring me here?"

CHAPTER 23

The taxi driver dropped his passengers at the train station in Cambridge. Dr. Easton had parked his car in a parking lot two blocks away. Dawson waited with the trunk. They had decided to pick up Easton's car in case the police or the men who had attacked the lab in Vernon questioned the taxi driver. They hoped their trail would end at the train station. This would buy them some time to discover the secret of the machine.

Dawson had dropped his satellite phone in the molten gold back at the lab. Now he had no way to contact Thomas. His telepathy powers did not come like the others. He could only communicate with Goode, but Goode had to originate the link. Dawson's scientific mind would not let him relax enough to believe thoughts could be transmitted through the air. He tried many times but nothing happened. Now he wished he could scream out thoughts to anyone who would listen. It was against the rules to use regular telephones for the business of the Brotherhood. The risks were too great. His only hope was to keep working on the machine until Goode contacted him.

Dr. Easton pulled his car up to the shuttle shelter. He and Dawson loaded the trunk in the back. The trunk had a slight vibration that neither man had noticed through all the excitement. Inside the car, Dawson breathed a sigh of relief. The two men continued the journey to Easton's lab.

"This is exciting. I think we are on the verge of a major breakthrough. The way the machine made the gold plate disappear and fused it into the van's roof is simply amazing. This defies physical science. I think we opened a wormhole. This is no laser," muttered Dr. Easton, almost out of breath while thinking about the possibilities. He started rambling about string theory and time travel to other dimensions.

"Enough. Calm down, Doctor! We are in danger here. Let's stay focused. Stay on your side of the road. You are weaving on the road like a drunk," cautioned Dawson.

"Okay, you're right. We don't need to get pulled over with this thing in our trunk. Yes, we need to get to my lab. First step, right?"

"That's it, Doc, one step at a time," responded Dawson. He wiped sweat from his forehead while looking out the side mirror to confirm that they were not being followed.

* * * * *

The campus was deserted. Easton was right about the tight security at his lab. The back gate had razor wire and military-style security 24-7. Cameras were everywhere. Dawson pulled his baseball cap over his eyes to avoid his picture being taken. Easton flashed his ID at the gate, and the guard pushed the button to let the car pass through the heavy steel gate.

"I see what you were talking about. Your lab is a secure facility."

"Yes, the university has a contract to develop prototypes for drone technology. My lab is not involved in the program, but I get the same security. Sometimes they call me in to consult, but mostly they leave me alone to tinker. They know I'm dying. The director pulled all of my projects and left me alone." Easton's voice turned sad as he thought about his health.

Easton parked, and Dawson got a cart to roll the trunk into the lab. Inside the facility, Dr. Easton got excited again. He turned on the lights and directed Dawson on where to place the trunk.

* * * * *

The commando raid on the farmhouse failed to produce the dagger. The GPS signals from the dagger case led Stark's men to the train station where Dawson and Easton left the van. The leader flashed one-hundred-dollar bills to porters and taxi drivers until he got the information needed to continue the search. The FBI was in close pursuit, armed with a description of the black SUVs and the masked commandos. A neighbor near Dawson's farm had reported this information to the authorities.

Stark's men ditched the SUVs at the next town and secured other transportation. Homeland Security put all of its resources in the chase because NASA had recorded a strange wave anomaly at the New Jersey farmhouse site. The government feared the worst, a possible terrorist attack in the form of a new weapon. The dead bodies at the farmhouse made the threat more real. It had been eighteen hours since Miss Erd had been taken. Stark's patience was running short. If his men did not retrieve the dagger soon, he would have to go through with an exchange of Erd for the dagger.

CHAPTER 24

Standing behind Rashe, viewing the images on the computer, everything became clear to Thomas. The ancient manuscripts recorded experiments conducted after men of science discovered a unique crystal from a meteorite. The crystal resembled quartz but had mysterious properties when exposed to high levels of sunlight. Rashe translated the text written in the margins. They had a major breakthrough with unlocking the secret of the stones during the siege of Granada, but ran out of time. The scribbled writing showed the stress of the author.

Rashe said, "The author of these three books is unknown. These books were found in an unmarked grave in Marrakesh during the construction of the toll road expansion. The bones of a hand in the grave were wrapped around these books, but nothing was found to identify the dead man."

"I believe Akin was one of the founders of the Brotherhood, and Jack may be his descendant." Thomas spoke to Rashe while looking at Jack. He continued, "We recovered the dagger three months ago. These books solved the puzzle of the origin of the dagger. The stones in the handle of the dagger were hidden to prevent the Spanish from finding the secrets the stones possess. The men who were here three days ago must also know about the meteorite, the mysterious stones, and the dagger's potential power. In the wrong hands, this power could turn the world upside down," said Thomas as he paced the floor, thinking about Erd.

"You know there were two identical daggers." Rashe turned to a page in the book to show him.

"Two daggers," said Thomas.

"If there are two daggers, then someone else is looking for the secret power of the object too. They may be running the same experiments as Dawson. If they have one of the daggers, why kidnap Erd?" Thomas said to Jack.

"They don't want to share power with anyone. It's about control. Do you think Dawson figured out the secret of the dagger? He needs to hurry. I think someone else is working on this too. If they figure out the secret, Erd's value to them will be diminished greatly. Whoever gets there first wins the prize," responded Jack as he looked out the window.

"Dawson can do it. He's missing now. I hope he's safe. He knows how important this is to the Brotherhood, and now it appears someone else knows the secret too," said Thomas.

Rashe said, "I've heard rumors about a secret African cult. So, you do exist. Many think you are myth and folklore, 'A dream of the fallen.'"

"We bleed and sweat just like you. We are real," said Thomas, looking out the window and wondering where Erd could be.

"As a child, my father's ghost stories about the men in the shadows looking over all of us seemed like fantasy. I have been waiting, watching, and planning and now I learn the Great Akin is one of your founders." Rashe closed his eyes for moment as he thought about the connection.

The room was quiet. Then Rashe jumped out of his chair. "You should hurry. Go to the sea to find your friend. Those men who were here earlier smelled of seaweed and Spanish wine. Ceuta and Melilla are autonomous Spanish cities surrounded by Morocco on the Mediterranean. Go find your friend and get after those evil men. You ride with the Great Akin!" Rashe downloaded the images of the three books on a flash drive and handed it to Thomas.

In that instant, an image of a lighthouse flashed in Thomas's mind with a brief thought from Erd saying, *Help me!*

Thomas asked Rashe, "Does either of these cities have a lighthouse?"

"Yes, Melilla has one."

Thomas called Zek and Jamal. "We need to search for Erd on the coast. Go to Melilla and find the lighthouse. Jack and I will join you. Call me when you get there."

Thomas looked into Rashe eyes. He said, "We are all on the same journey."

"Peace be with you, brother. I will keep your secret. Go well, my friend," responded Rashe as he hugged Jack.

Reluctantly, Jack smiled and nodded. "Whatever, we will see this through, Akin or not."

Salman helped Jack gather his things, and the three men left the archive in the Range Rover, driving down the mountain toward Marrakesh. "Marrakesh is five hundred kilometers from Melilla. It will take over eight hours to drive," said Salman as he drove the Rover through the winding roads down the Atlas Mountains.

"That's too long. Erd could be dead in four hours," said Jack, studying the map for the route back to the city.

"I have an uncle who can fly you there. He has a plane in Marrakesh. He is a good pilot. He flew for the government until he got too old to pass the test," said Salman.

"And he still flies?" asked Thomas, looking at Jack.

"Yes, it was political. They pushed him out. His plane is on a private airstrip outside the city. He had an import business on the side, and the government did not approve of his customers," Salman said, raising his hands in the air.

"Sounds like he may be a smuggler," said Jack.

"My friend, I would not tell you wrong. My grandfather was a pilot in the war with Germany. He flew for the French when Morocco was a colony. Grandfather was a hero pilot with medals and everything. After Morocco gained its independence, France stopped paying grandfather his pension. That was not right. Papa fought to free France. They owed him. My uncle still remembers how the French government treated Papa, so he does not trust any government. Uncle always says to prepare for the unexpected. He is a good man. Do you want to go to Melilla or not?" responded Salman.

"Call him. See if he can take us, we will decide when we see his plane." Thomas looked at his watch and worried about Erd. He thought they were running out of time.

Salman smiled, "Good, you will see. This will work. He will get you there quickly. Melilla's customs officers are strict, but he can get you in the city without any trouble."

Jack and Thomas sat silently as the Range Rover bounded over potholes onto the main road. Thomas sent a text message to the *Scorpion*, his command ship, and ordered it to sail to Melilla and anchor twenty miles off the coast. The captain replied with an ETA of four hours. The hulking fishing trawler fired up its two huge engines and quickly left Casablanca in the distance as it sailed for the Strait of Gibraltar.

CHAPTER 25

A courier arrived at Goode's hotel in St. Petersburg just before dusk. The front desk sent a message for Goode to sign for the package. Inside was the duplicate dagger. At the urging of the elders, Thomas had ordered a replica to be made of the original dagger given to Dawson. The elders warned that others would be seeking the ancient object. Goode knew it was not the real dagger. It was made of gold and had precious stones, but that was all. The Brotherhood would never trade its legacy for any price. He hoped it would be enough to convince the Russians that he had the real dagger to trade for Erd.

Napoli's driver was waiting in the lobby when Goode came down to sign for the package brought by the courier. After Goode took possession of the package, the driver motioned for Goode to come speak to him. "Mr. Chenko sent this picture for you to see," said the driver holding up his phone to show Goode a video. The video image was of Erd shackled in a chair and talking in a monotone voice, drugged, holding the *London Times* newspaper with that day's date. The driver said, "This is proof of life. We go now?"

Goode nodded as he placed the package in his leather briefcase with the carrying strap over his shoulder. Goode had the gun Napoli gave him in his pocket. He wrapped his scarf over his neck, put on his gloves, and followed the driver to the car.

It had been eighteen hours since Erd had been taken. Seeing her alive made Goode hopeful that they could get her back. He called Thomas. "Erd is alive. I just saw the proof of life video. I am en route to negotiate the trade for the dagger."

"Keep the negotiations going. If they discover the dagger is a fake, they will kill her. We have a lead on where they may be holding her, so buy us some time. Stall on setting up the meeting for the exchange. Show them the dagger but do not let them handle it." Thomas hung up the phone.

The car slowed to a halt due to traffic. Goode noticed people running on the sidewalk. Gunfire erupted and then the windshield of the car exploded as several bullets whizzed by Goode's head, killing the driver. The car crashed into a parked vehicle and rolled to a stop. A man dressed in a police uniform approached with his gun drawn and ordered Goode out of the car. Goode knew they were after the dagger. He fired the gun Napoli had given him, wounding the policeman, and then climbed over the seat, pushing the body of the driver out of the door. The wounded policeman fired several more shots at Goode, who wrestled with the steering wheel as he tried to drive the car away from danger.

A few blocks away, he continued to check the rearview mirror. However, there was no sign of anyone following him. Goode drove the car into the basement of a parking garage. He found a blanket in the trunk and spread it over the bloodstained seat, then walked to a nearby hotel. Goode's hands were shaking. Blood was on his gloves and his coat. He finally checked to see if he had been shot. Goode was relieved that the blood was from the driver. He thought about leaving the driver's body in the street. He panicked. It had all happened so fast, he'd acted on instincts alone. Goode hoped Napoli would understand.

Inside the hotel, Goode called Napoli. "The driver is dead, killed by a man in a policeman's uniform!"

"Where are you? I will come to you. These pigs have no honor." Napoli started cussing in Russian.

"I am at the Red Square hotel in the bar," responded Goode with his coat in his hand. He was afraid the blood would draw unwanted attention.

"I will be there in ten minutes." Napoli hung up.

Goode ordered vodka to calm his nerves. He studied his watch as the minutes passed while waiting for Napoli to arrive. He thought about Dawson and tried to link his thoughts with him.

* * * * *

Jamal's shoulder wound had finally stopped bleeding. He drank the last of the olive oil and the pain faded. The trail following the sniper's jeep ran cold ten miles from the burned-out cargo plane. Travel to the city of Mellila required a charter flight for Zek and Jamal. This time Zek decided it was better to lease a plane to give them more flexibility for their search for Erd. Zek had his international pilot's license, and he was certified as a commercial pilot for helicopter and multiengine aircraft. After the military, he started an air cargo service until the money ran out from his savings. That was when Erd found him in Rio.

The pilot who flew Zek and Jamal from Alexandria, Egypt, was losing money on his private charter service. He and Zek had a lot in common. When Zek and Jamal returned to Casablanca International Airport, Zek approached the pilot with an offer to rent his plane for forty-eight hours. After some negotiations and a five-thousand-dollar payment, the plane was theirs. The pilot filed flight plans for Zek and helped with customs for the trip as a cargo charter, which allowed Jamal to register his guns as cargo.

Jamal, looking at Zek in the captain's chair said, "I'm not ready to die, brother." He had never sat in the copilot's seat. "This is too close to the action."

"It's just like driving a car," said Zek.

"Yeah right, just don't fall asleep. Where are the brakes on this thing?"

"I will walk you through the controls once we are in the air. You will be flying like a pro in no time," responded Zek. He flipped buttons on the control panel, readying for takeoff. Jamal braced himself for the flight. He could hear his heart beating loudly. He glanced over at Zek to see if he could hear the pounding. Zek calmly taxied the plane down the runway then off they went in the air, smoothly climbing through the clouds. Jamal's eyes were big enough to burst.

Zek said, "Relax, the takeoff and landing are the most dangerous parts of flying, we are halfway there."

Jamal nodded and settled back with the flight plan in his hand. He said, "I'm ready to work. Show me how to fly this thing."

CHAPTER 26

Dr. Easton studied the video from the last experiment at the farm and confirmed his suspicions about the machine. He put the flash drive in the USB port of a large monitor in the lab to show Dawson. He slowed the image in a frame-by-frame shot and then switched to slow motion. He said, "See the gold plate here on the monitor? The image starts to fade and reappear, then breaks into particles but keeps its form. It's like the atoms take an individual form then a vacuum swallows the particles. Then the plate reappeared in the roof of the van. I am convinced we opened a wormhole in the lab. It may still be open. Based on my calculations, the energy pulse would take eight to ten hours to dissipate the wormhole."

"But why send the plate into the roof of the van? Why not to another dimension or a thousand miles away? I don't understand," responded Dawson as he replayed the video again.

"Yes, it is a mystery, but it happened. We need to find a way to control the outcome. The van's monitor may have had some gold filaments, but who knows?" Easton said, grunting while placing the heavy machine on a table. Near the table, he positioned a light panel to power the device. "The quartz stones are glowing. They must still be charged from the sunlight. We probably need only a little light to charge the device to run the machine again," mumbled Easton as he powered up the lights to test the lumens. He continued, "We must try again. I think I know how to miniaturize the device. I have all the components. We may be able to control the machine with a brain machine interface to direct the outcome."

Dr. Easton went to his office and brought back a black box. He opened the case and pulled out a metallic helmet that was fitted with wires and Light-emitting diodes (LED) lights. He said, "I have been experimenting with brain wave sensory control to turn lights on and type messages on the computer. This is a prototype that will ultimately enable pilots to fly unmanned aerial vehicles or drone aircraft with their thoughts. The brain emits electromagnetic waves. This helmet magnifies the brainwaves to allow thoughts to control certain devices. This machine is controlled by electromagnetic energy. If we use this helmet, you, theoretically, should be able to control where the object is transported. I think I can retrofit a miniature version of the laser device into the helmet. Let me try."

Dawson, shaking his head, said, "Okay, but this thing could theoretically fry your brain, too. This is risky."

"Where is your sense of adventure?" Easton laughed. "Besides, I have safeguards built into the device. The current is only allowed to go one way, from the mind to the machine. Three redundant sensors will block any current flowing back to the brain and break the connection. Of course, there is some risk, but we are running out of time." Dr. Easton flipped a switch and the helmet vibrated. The LED lights flashed red and then went to a solid green.

"I don't know about this, Dr. Easton. All of this is untested." Dawson walked away. He paced the floor, not knowing what to do. At that moment, Goode connected with Dawson with a mind link. Excited, Dawson started speaking aloud to Goode instead of using his thoughts. He said, "My phone is damaged. I could not contact anyone. We left the lab and then heard there was a shootout at the facility. We are on the run with the dagger and the machine. I need help—"

"Slow down. Use your mind to communicate. Erd is still alive, but I think she's been drugged. They're after the dagger. I'm in negotiations to exchange a duplicate dagger for her, but I think they found out your location from Erd," said Goode.

"Yes, we found a GPS sensor in the dagger case. If Erd gave them the frequency and the code, then they probably tracked our location in New Jersey. We are close to a breakthrough, but it's risky." Dawson stopped talking. Dr. Easton was looking at him strangely but then started working on retrofitting the machine into the helmet.

"Go buy a disposable phone and dial this number. I will send your number to Thomas. He will call you. We are running out of time. Do what you need to do." Goode terminated the mind link.

Dawson prepared to leave Dr. Easton's laboratory. He said, "When I return, we will try the drone pilot helmet. It better work or at least not kill me." He pulled the baseball hat down over his eyes. Dawson's anxiety eased as the vehicle cleared security to leave the facility.

* * * * *

Kaiya's trip through the wormhole created another seismic wave recorded by NASA. The sensitive equipment monitoring the dairy farm set off an alarm, causing the army to deploy troops around the farmhouse. The Department of Defense took over for the FBI. Green camouflaged trucks lined the gravel road leading to the site. Helicopters circled above. Dr. McLeay's phone never stopped ringing. He didn't know the cause of the seismic waves or what had happened to his colleague.

It had been an hour since Kaiya arrived at the lighthouse. Sitting in the dark, tied to a chair, her mind raced with thoughts of probabilities. Her training as a scientist helped her mind focus on how she had traveled to the location. A faint whisper would occasionally interrupt her thoughts. It started with a murmur and then random images would appear in her mind. Kaiya noticed the interruption happened when Erd would fade in and out of consciousness. The faint scent of vanilla aroused Erd's senses.

Finally, a voice asked, "Who are you?"

"Who are you?" asked Kaiya in a whisper

"I am Erd. How did you get here?"

"I don't know. I was in New Jersey at a farmhouse, then I appeared here," responded Kaiya.

"New Jersey? Did you see Dawson? Did he send you?"

"Everyone was dead. There was a shootout. Several people fled. Someone took a machine with them. I suspect they are responsible for my being here," whispered Kaiya, feeling strange talking to the woman through her thoughts.

"Don't tell them. They will kill you if they learn you know about the machine."

The guard entered the room, loaded Erd on the cart, and rolled her back for more questions. The IV drip stopped when the bottle was empty. Kaiya stared in horror, thinking she would be next. She knew she would talk. Sweat rolled down her forehead. When the door closed, she struggled with the bindings on her hand until one became free. Her phone was in her pocket. The guard hadn't searched her well. She dialed the number for Dr. McLeay. The line was busy, she got the voice mail. "It's me, Kaiya. I'm in danger. Men with guns have me tied up at a lighthouse. I don't know where I am. Help me!" she screamed.

The guard returned as she finished the call. He punched Kaiya in the stomach and grabbed the phone. He threw the phone against the wall and slapped her face, knocking the chair over on its side. Kaiya was out cold. He re-tied her hands and taped her mouth. The guard dreaded telling Stark about the phone call; he knew it could mean his life.

CHAPTER 27

The Range Rover came to a stop on an abandoned airstrip. Grass and weeds had taken over much of the runway. Thomas looked at Jack. He shook his head then looked at his watch as he thought of the precious little time they had to save Erd. They sat in silence, afraid to say a word, hoping that Salman would be able to deliver on his promise.

"What time is it?" Salman inquired as he opened his door and looked up at the sky.

"One forty-five," Jack answered quickly, having just checked his watch.

Thomas said nothing. He had gotten out of the Rover before Salman and started pacing back and forth, kicking stones to see how far they would go. Finally, Thomas said, "Salman, are you sure about your uncle? This is very important."

"Quiet," Salman said, straining to hear something. Then there was a low hum, which grew louder, until Salman said, "Look! There's his plane. See, my uncle is here. He is always on time."

A large dust cloud roared up the runway, and Thomas and Jack ducked behind the Rover until the plane came to a stop. Salman covered his face with his turban to watch the plane land. He ran over to greet his uncle as he disembarked from the plane. His uncle was a huge man, possibly three hundred pounds, with a long unkempt gray beard. He had a gun shoulder holster and knife on his side belt. Salman and the huge bearded man embraced then walked over to Thomas.

"You want to go to Mellila today?"

"Yes, we need to get there as soon as possible," responded Thomas.

"I do not carry drugs in my plane. If I find you have drugs, I will cut your throats and dump your bodies in the sea," Salman's uncle said as he drew his large knife to sharpen it while they talked.

"No drugs. We need safe passage to Mellila. You can check our bags if you'd like," said Thomas as he tossed a package of one-hundred-dollar bills at the pilot. He continued, "That's five thousand dollars for the trip, and there will be a bonus if you get us there with no problems. We don't want to go through customs and immigration, if you know what I mean."

"Can you swim?" asked the pilot.

"Yes," answered Jack. "Why?"

"We will need to slip into Mellila on the coast. I can land on the water, but you will have to swim to shore. It's not far, but the waters are rough." The pilot looked suspiciously at Thomas as he counted the money.

Salman said, "I will come with you." He looked at Thomas to assure him that everything would go as promised.

"How long will it take to get there?"

"Three to four hours. If we catch a tailwind out of the mountains, it may be sooner."

Thomas looked at Jack, then nodded. "Let's get this show on the road. We're burning daylight."

The pilot walked around the Cessna 208 Caravan with Jack. The plane had seen better days. The pilot explained that the plane was built in the 1980s as an amphibian transport for the military and was sold at auction ten years ago. He said, "She is a real beauty and smooth as silk in the air." He patted the engine as they walked. His eyes livened up as he talked about the plane.

Thomas was on the phone with Zek, discussing their plans to rendezvous in Melilla. Jack and Salman unloaded the Range Rover and boarded the plane. The plane's engine crackled, then turned into a smooth hum as the four men settled in for the flight to the Spanish city.

CHAPTER 28

Stark's men searched Dr. Easton's house, ripping up the sofa and clearing the book selves to find anything that would lead them to the dagger. They found his lab ID for the laboratory at MIT. The leader called Stark. "We searched the doctor's house. We found nothing. He may be at work."

"Find him. I'm running out of time."

"If we break into the laboratory, the government authorities will know."

"Do it. Leave no one alive to talk."

"That will cost extra."

The cleaning lady walked into the open garage door and was startled by masked men with guns. She pushed the panic button on the alarm panel. The commando leader slit her throat.

He ordered, "Load up! Put the body in the freezer. Move now! The police will be here soon."

* * * * *

An hour had passed since Dawson returned with the disposable phone. Dawson made contact with Thomas to update him on the progress with the dagger. "I will send you some help, but there is no guarantee they will get to you in time. You are on your own for now. If you think you may be captured, destroy the machine. Understood?" Thomas waited for Dawson's reply.

"Understood," Dawson said then terminated the call.

Dr. Easton ignored Dawson, who was pacing the floor. He busily worked on the helmet unit to control the machine. He had completed the finishing touches on the miniature version of the laser that would fit into the helmet.

The lab phone rang. A voice asked, "Is this Dr. Easton?"

"Yes."

"You have a burglar alarm ringing at your home. The police are on the way to check it out."

Doctor Easton hung up the phone. He said, "Dawson, I think they broke into my house, looking for us. That was the security company calling about the alarm. We don't have much time. They will come here next. We need to finish and test the device."

"How did they find your house?"

"I lost my driver's license at the farmhouse... they may have found it." Easton turned on the power switch on the helmet to test the circuit. The lights flashed on the front panel where he installed the quartz stones from the dagger.

Dawson finished dismantling the original laser device they had built at the farmhouse in New Jersey. He secured the dagger in his messenger bag. He said, "I hope you're right about this helmet. You might fry my brains with this thing."

"Trust me. It will work. I tested all the circuits. You should be able to control the machine's reaction with your thoughts. When you open the wormhole, that is another story. We don't know where you may end up."

"That's what worries me," said Dawson.

"This is exciting," said Dr. Easton, smiling and looking at the monitor, testing the wavelength from the helmet while Dawson tried it on. "Let's test the laser to see if you can control where the gold plate goes this time. My modifications should allow you to control where the wormhole opens and closes. Where the hole closes is where the plate will land."

Dawson's heart was beating faster as he thought about having an experimental device wired to his brain with the helmet. He slowed down his breathing to listen to Dr. Easton's directions. Easton handed him a device that controlled the electronics in the helmet. The helmet visor screen had a built-in display where Dawson could see the countdown for the test.

"One, two, three…ten. Go! Press the red button and think of the table to the right of the door," yelled Dr. Easton. "Press the button now!"

Dawson pressed the button. The lights on the helmet blinked red to green. The screen on his visor flashed the countdown sequence. He said, "Eight, nine, ten…here we go!"

Moments later, the solid gold plate disappeared and then reappeared on the table near the door. Dawson powered down the helmet and breathed a sigh of relief that his brain hadn't fried as a result of the test. Dr. Easton placed a vase where the gold plate was located. The vase disappeared and reappeared on the table like the gold plate had earlier. He said, "The wormhole is still open. Amazing! It will collapse soon."

"What does this mean?" asked Dawson.

"Unlimited possibilities," said Easton.

A loud explosion rang out from the direction of the security checkpoint at the lab entrance. The alarm sounded. "Intruder Alert! Intruder Alert!" Automatic gunfire could be heard approaching Dr. Easton's lab. Another explosion shook the walls. The ceiling tiles fell to the floor.

"They will be here soon. You need to go. Turn the helmet on and enlarge the target field to include yourself. I will stall them to give you more time. Go. Go now!" screamed Dr. Easton.

"But…I don't know how to operate this without you. I, I—"

"Son, you can do this. I taught you, remember? Take this flash drive. It has all my notes on the device and some improvements I didn't incorporate yet. My time is over. Your secret is safe with me. Go now!" Dr. Easton turned on the power switch. He yelled, "Think about a pleasant place and go there now."

An explosion blew the door open. A dust cloud pushed Dr. Easton back, and there was smoke everywhere. Dawson powered the device and disappeared into thin air.

Dr. Easton went to the door, stood in front of Stark's commandos, and said, "May, I help you?"

The leader asked, "Where's the dagger?"

"Could you describe it? Maybe I can help you find—"

The commando leader shot Dr. Easton in the head, and brains spattered against the wall. The leader pushed his body out of the way. He had no time for conversation. Dr. Easton had accomplished his lifelong dream with science and helped his friend escape.

Government security forces were on the loud speaker. "We have your position surrounded. Put down your weapons." Footsteps could be heard running up the hall. The *zap, zap, zip, zip* of gunfire filled the air. There would be no surrender. Stark's men knew the score. Several tear gas canisters exploded through the door. The smoke was thick. Men with gas masks and red laser-target beams showed through the smoke. The order was to take the terrorists alive, but dead was okay too.

The leader of the commando squad searched the lab for the dagger, but only found the case. He planted C4 explosives near the back wall of Easton's lab and blew open a hole that led to the parking lot so he and his men could make their escape. The explosion rocked the building; smoke and debris were scattered everywhere. A van screeched its tires to a stop in the parking lot. Two commandos were dead. The leader and three men dove into the moving van.

* * * * *

The alarm sounded again at JPL's monitoring station. Another seismic wave was targeted in Cambridge, Massachusetts, at the MIT research center. The army was there searching for terrorists responsible for blowing up the security checkpoint and killing four private security guards at the gate. Army investigators were on-site when they got the call to respond to the threat of the seismic wave.

The officer in charge answered the phone. "Sir, we have nine dead, including two terrorists and three of our men wounded. The scene is not good; three scientists were killed as far as we can see. We are securing the perimeter. An unknown number of terrorists escaped capture. That is all I have to report, sir."

The NSA director said, "Do not let anyone in the lab. It's not safe. There is a seismic wave still present at your current position. This happened earlier today in New Jersey, and we lost personnel to some unexplained phenomenon. Be careful. We are sending personnel from NASA to investigate."

Dr. McLeay's phone was ringing every two seconds. He finally answered the call from the White House. "Yes sir."

"Don't speak, listen. You now report to me." The voice of the national security adviser left no opportunity for questions. "This is a presidential order. Whatever you find out about the seismic wave, you call me first. Understand?"

"Yes, sir. What do I tell my boss and the army?"

"Tell them to call me if they have any questions." He hung up the phone.

Dr. McLeay was most worried about his missing assistant, Kaiya. *How could she just vanish in thin air?* he thought.

His car came to a stop outside the lab at MIT. The media was waiting for him to give a statement before he entered the facility. A podium had been hurriedly assembled for him to give the official account of what had happened. The FBI went first, with the announcement of a successful disruption of a terrorist attack.

Dr. McLeay's statement followed. "We offer high praise for the FBI and other government security agents for securing this facility and preserving vital technology for our green energy program."

His statement about green energy puzzled the press. He didn't answer any questions and rushed inside under heavy security. Dr. McLeay didn't know what else to say. Taking orders from the White House, and the Pentagon, required him to walk a fine line. His phone started ringing again. He ignored all calls except for one. It was a call from Kaiya, his assistant. Before he could answer, the call went to voice mail. *She's alive*, he thought. The terrorists must have her. Excited, he rushed over to the agent in command and turned the message over to the FBI. He went to work in the lab in hopes of finding a clue of what technology could cause the wave anomaly and take his assistant. Dr. McLeay disappeared within minutes of walking into the lab. The wormhole was still open. The army sealed off the area as they had at the farmhouse. Now there were two missing scientists along with a score of dead bodies, and the government had no answers.

CHAPTER 29

Before his death, Frederick Eddington had made several calls during his flight to Paris to recover the diamonds he thought were hidden in red fish containers. Eddington, the former director of the International Bureau of Commerce, was obsessed with searching for egg-shaped diamonds from an ancient Mali Kingdom. Eddington was on the trail of Thomas Jet, Miss Erd, and Jamal in the Gulf of Mexico when he made a call to the Russian, Napoli. Eddington had bragged of a large collection of diamonds that would soon be in his possession. He offered Napoli ten percent of the deal if he arranged for the cutting of selected stones. Napoli and Eddington had done business many times before, using blood diamonds to elude the Kimberly Process, which prohibited trade in African conflict diamonds. The appearance of Goode in Hong Kong with large diamonds got Napoli's attention.

A month later, Goode had traveled to Hong Kong to complete a transaction for brokerage services for the distinctive blue diamonds he'd recovered in Belize. He arranged the transaction using several shell corporations to conceal the true source of the precious stones. After the deal was completed, Goode traveled by ferry to Macau with his business associate to celebrate the new venture. The chance meeting with Napoli at the Hong Kong diamond conference and again in the hotel lounge in Macau had worried Goode.

Goode had given Napoli his pinky ring after spending hours talking about Russia and his hometown, St.

Petersburg. Napoli promised to make introductions for Goode with several influential diamond cutters in St. Petersburg. As a goodwill gesture, Goode gave Napoli his ring.

"That African stole my diamonds, and now he wants to sell them back to me," shouted Napoli to his boss.

"You know this to be true?"

"No, I do not have any proof, but the coincidence of them having such large stones after I got a call from my supplier cannot be ignored," said Napoli.

"Napoli, we stand to make a lot of money with these diamonds. Regardless of who possesses them, we get twenty percent. You know the rules. Whoever possesses the stones owns them. There is nothing gained from turning the African deal sour. You have no proof. He could take his diamonds to Israel and cut us out totally," said the man with tattoos on his neck and hands. He blew smoke from his cigar into Napoli's face. He continued, "This is business, not personal."

"These are my diamonds. We could have all the diamonds. I can feel it," responded Napoli as he looked at the ring Goode had given him.

"You risk more than diamonds if you ruin this deal. The shipment is due tomorrow. The funds are in a bank escrow account. We cannot get our money back if you screw this up. Do not speak of this to me again." The crime boss stood up from the sofa in the private meeting room. The door opened to let in the sounds of the girls and music from the dance floor below. The Equinox was closed for a private party for the Penquse crime family.

Angry, Napoli left the meeting and did not join the festivities. He went to the office. His phone rang. It was Goode calling to tell him his driver had been killed.

"Where are you? I will come to you. Those pigs have no honor," responded Napoli. He smiled as he thought that soon all the diamonds would be his.

Inside the Red Square Hotel, Goode sat at the bar, feeling very alone for the first time since he'd joined the Brotherhood. Erd's voice had been silenced. He feared she would be dead soon. The secrets of the dagger could be lost to terrorists, and he was alone in a foreign country being hunted by those he feared might be the police. He kept thinking about why the Russians would be involved with Erd's kidnapping. *It must be the diamonds they are after*, he thought.

CHAPTER 30

An hour into Zek and Jamal's flight, the powder blue sky surrounded the cargo plane. Zek gave Jamal some instruction and let him take the controls. The plane dipped abruptly.

"Steady, steady bring up the nose. Stay on this heading. See the arrow? Keep it right there," said Zek, pointing at the control panel as he shuffled the charts for the flight plan.

"This is cool. I can do this," responded Jamal, and then he looked out the window. "When I lost consciousness after I bumped my head on the ceiling in the slave castle, I dreamed I was a slave about to be shipped out. It felt so real, down to the whip's lashes on my back. I felt the blood, pain, and misery. I called out for you to come get me. I was afraid I would never wake up."

"Wow. That dream was strange. It was enough for me just to see the conditions and hear the history. Yeah, I don't need to do that again," responded Zek as he looked up from the map.

"No lie, but I am glad we went. Our brothers and sisters were herded like cattle into the dungeon, while upstairs their captors attended church. If that's Christian behavior, then I want no parts of that kind of Christianity. The Spanish and Portuguese were good Catholics, right? We must never forget what happened." Tears came to Jamal's eyes. He thought of the moments in his dream when he was shackled to five brothers in the slave dungeon.

"You can't blame slavery on Christianity. Man made the decision to profit from human bondage; it's not about religion, though I understand what you mean. Let's focus on our mission to find Erd. We will be landing in twenty minutes," said Zek while looking through the custom's forms. "This is Spanish territory we're entering. I'll take control for the rest of the flight."

"A Spanish city surrounded by Morocco. You know there is a story behind this. Let's get on the ground." Jamal went to the back of the plane to check the weapons and other equipment against the customs' forms.

The control tower came on the speaker and provided clearance for landing.

* * * * *

Dawson tumbled for one hundred yards, rolling downhill until a large boulder stopped his momentum. The helmet had a built-in GPS processor on the view screen. He was a little dot near Lexington, Kentucky. Dazed from the journey through the wormhole, he pulled off the helmet and stumbled down to a creek. He submerged his head into water and drank as much as he could swallow. He thought, *Kentucky of all places. "Bluegrass country." It was all I could think of with the gunfire and explosions in the lab. Dr. Easton said to go somewhere safe. This is where I grew up. I always felt safe here.*

Moments later, Dr. McLeay came tumbling down the hill. He was unconscious. Dawson ran over to see if he was alive. He checked his pulse and his identification.

He said, "NASA JPL laboratory. How did they know where we were? Can they track this device?"

Dawson didn't want to be around when McLeay woke up. Though he had plenty of questions, he was afraid others would be coming through the wormhole. He remembered Dr. Easton said the hole might stay open for a few minutes or hours. Dawson grabbed the helmet and ran to a nearby farmhouse. He found a gym bag to put the helmet in then hitched a ride into town. He needed to contact Thomas. Dawson was afraid. If he used the machine again, he would be followed.

CHAPTER 31

Stark was out of the green fluid for the IV drip that kept Erd sedated. Now, sodium pentothal was all he had to make her talk. The twenty-four hours were almost up. He received word that his men had failed to recover the dagger in the States. The trail was cold, and his men were on the run, heading for Canada. Stark needed Erd alive to trade. The phone call made by Kaiya interrupted Starks' interrogation of Erd. They searched Kaiya again and discovered her badge from the JPL laboratory in Maryland.

"Maryland. Really? How did you end up here?" asked Stark with a smile on his face.

Kaiya said nothing at first then said, "I don't know?"

"Good. We can help you with your memory. Don't worry. We will know everything soon." Stark pointed to his men to remove her shirt. He yelled, "Take it off. Tie her hands tight and her feet too. You fools let her make a phone call. Who did she call?"

He punched the guard who brought her in then he rammed his knife through his heart. As the man fell to the ground, blood sprayed on Kaiya's face. She cried and screamed, "Don't kill me!"

"Gag her," Stark shouted as he ran his fingers over her breast. "This is going to hurt you more than me." He jammed the needle into her arm and filled her vein with truth serum, then he waited for the chemical to do its work. Erd was in a chair in the corner, watching in horror as an enraged Stark again stabbed the dead guard's body.

Kaiya passed out from fear. Ammonia was used to revive her once the drug had made its way to her brain.

"Remove the gag," commanded Stark. "What's your name?"

"Kaiya Renee Nelson," she answered.

"Who did you call?"

"My boss, Dr. McLeay."

"What did you tell him?"

"I do not remember."

Stark punched her in the stomach then repeated, "What did you tell him?"

"I said help, there are men with guns. I'm at a lighthouse."

"Where is the lighthouse?" Stark asked

"I don't know." She started crying again.

Stark punched her again in the stomach. She doubled over, crying, "I don't know where I am." Then she passed out.

The ammonia was applied to her nose. She regained her composure. Stark asked, "How did you get here?"

"I don't know. I was in New Jersey at a farmhouse, then I was here," she said in a robotic tone.

Stark said, "New Jersey farmhouse? Take her away. I will finish with her later." He forgot about Erd. The drugs were wearing off. Erd was regaining control over her thoughts. Stark left the room to call the commando squad leader. The farmhouse in New Jersey puzzled him. He needed answers before resuming his questioning of Kaiya.

Erd reached out for Thomas in her mind. Tears ran down her cheeks. *Help me. I'm being held at a lighthouse. They will know soon about the dagger, Dawson, and the machine. Hurry, sweetheart.*

Thomas felt her presence. Erd's thoughts warmed his heart. He loved her. They were still almost two hours away from Melilla. Thomas called Jamal, "When you land, look for a lighthouse. They're holding Erd in a lighthouse," he repeated.

"We are making our final approach; we should be on the ground shortly. I'll let you know when we are clear of customs," responded Jamal.

Thomas was relieved. They were almost there. It had been twenty-two hours since Erd had been taken. *She is still alive,* he thought.

Jack said nothing to Thomas. He yelled to the pilot, "Does this plane go any faster?"

"If we go faster we may run low on fuel."

"No, stay the course. We need to get there in one piece." Jack started cleaning his gun and checking the ammunition.

Thomas sent a message to his command ship, the *Scorpion*, to send a boat to meet them in the Melilla Harbor.

CHAPTER 32

Dr. McLeay phoned the national security director at the White House from a pay phone. "I'm in Kentucky, nine hundred miles from Boston. I got here in a blink of an eye. Don't ask me how, but someone has figured out how to open and control wormholes. Teleportation is possible. Could you send someone to pick me up? I think I have a concussion."

The voice on the other side asked, "How could they do this without us knowing about it?"

"My assistant, Kaiya, suspected a wormhole when we reported the first seismic wave. Whoever has this technology is improving the control and distance as we speak. I suspect a hybrid laser. The lab at MIT attacked by terrorists today had a Dr. Easton who was responsible for drone guidance systems research. His project specialty was brain machine interface technology. Easton wrote several papers on advanced laser physics. We're not sure of his connection with the farmhouse attack in New Jersey. Dr. Easton is dead. He may have had an assistant. If they use the device again, we can track where they originate but not where they go. That's all we know," responded Dr. McLeay.

"Tell no one. We must keep this secret. This could start a new arms race if news of this device leaks out. No one must know." He hung up the phone and scrambled a military plane to pick up McLeay in Kentucky.

The FBI determined the dead terrorists were Russian ex-military from the tattoos found on their bodies. The national security director feared the Russians may already have the mysterious device.

Dawson boarded a bus to Nashville. He called Thomas. "It works. We miniaturized the process to fit in a helmet. Dr. Easton designed the modifications. He's dead. The terrorists killed him. I think the government can track the device at the origin point of the wormhole but not the end point. I'm on the run. A government official from JPL followed me through the wormhole. I left him unconscious in Kentucky. They don't know we have the device, yet."

"Great. Dawson, I knew you could figure it out. I will have the Obsidians send a team to meet you in Nashville."

"The Obsidians? I thought they stayed in the shadows to keep us in line. They're assassins, right?"

"Relax. They do special missions, too. I think you will sleep better knowing they are watching your back," said Thomas.

"Okay, but I heard they took out Pete," responded Dawson.

"Keep your head down; they will meet the bus. Tell no one about the device, not even the Obsidians. We need to get you out of the country. When you are in the clear, call me," Thomas terminated the call. He sent a text message to arrange for the team to meet Dawson. Only the elders could direct the Obsidians in the field. It had been like that since the beginning. Maalik called it a checks and balance system of power within the Brotherhood.

On the back of his bus ticket, Dawson scribbled notes for adjusting the wavelength of the device to avoid detection. He patted his backpack to check for the dagger. After confirming it was safely tucked away, he drifted to sleep.

CHAPTER 33

A black Mercedes sedan moved slowly in rush-hour traffic. Napoli was in deep thought when his mobile phone rang.

"We have trouble. We failed to retrieve the object. I must move forward with the trade for the woman. They may have developed a weapon from information contained in the dagger," said Stark. "The secret may be gone. My boss will kill me if he learns this."

"Stop talk of bosses. We will be the bosses soon. I want the diamonds and the weapon," shouted Napoli.

"You are a crazy man. Your life will end with talk like that. They could be listening," said Stark in a low voice.

"You brought this plan to me with talk of diamonds and secret weapons. There is no turning back. Let me worry about my life. I will be boss soon. We will negotiate the girl for the knife. When the Africans hand over the dagger, you give the woman to me. I'll be boss then." Napoli drank more vodka.

"I want no part of this." Stark hung up the phone.

* * * * *

Goode paced the floor in the hotel bar. Napoli walked in and ordered two vodkas. He drank the first glass before Goode approached him. He drank the second glass and then ordered the bottle. He said, "We drink now."

"No drink. We need to get my friend back. I have the dagger." Goode raised his shoulder bag to show the package with the object.

"We drink now." Napoli poured another glass and drank the vodka.

"What's wrong? Let's go." Goode started to pace the floor again.

"Let them kill her. She is not worth trouble." Napoli drank another glass. "I will help you for the diamonds. I take half. You have half. Good no?"

"What? I have no diamond deal with you. I negotiated my deal with the bank and Degel Diamond Ltd this morning. What are you talking about?" Goode started backing away, sensing something was about to go very badly.

Napoli started laughing. "I make a joke. Funny no? Let's go."

"What joke? I thought you were serious. Not very funny." Goode picked up his bloodstained coat. He reached in the pocket for the gun and placed it in his jacket pocket.

Napoli's icy blue eyes looked deadly, like they had when he shot the second-in-command mob boss the day before. He shot him dead without a thought. Napoli took the bottle with him. The bartender didn't question him about paying, as he knew better.

The ride to the meeting was eerie. Napoli drank several glasses of vodka and then said, "Did you steal the diamonds you sell now?"

"Steal? What are you talking about, steal?" Goode had his hand on the gun in his pocket.

Napoli laughed. "You know steal. I steal all the time. It's nothing. It's very profitable."

"I stole nothing. What's going on here? What are you saying?" demanded Goode.

Laughing, Napoli said, "You are too serious, my friend. Relax. It's okay. Say it."

"I stole nothing. Stop the car. Let me out here. Stop the car, now!" ordered Goode. The car came to a stop. Goode opened the door.

"If you leave this car, you are no longer my friend. I cannot protect you. This is a dangerous city." Napoli rolled up his window and drove off. Napoli knew the dagger Goode had in his possession was a fake and of no value to him. There was no need to play the game anymore.

* * * * *

Goode didn't return to his hotel. He felt his life was in danger. Napoli had as much as said he was going to kill him. *They never intended to trade the dagger for Erd*, Goode thought. *This was all a charade.*

Goode called Thomas. "They're going to kill Erd. They never intended to trade the dagger for her. They were stalling. They're after the diamonds too."

"Dawson has the machine operational. They know it. The dagger is useless to them. They're coming after us. It's time to come home," said Thomas.

Napoli sent his men to Goode's hotel with an order to kill him on sight. St. Petersburg suddenly became a more dangerous city. Later that evening, the body of Napoli's boss was dumped in the Neva River. The body was missing fingertips and teeth. The Penquse crime family had a new boss: Mr. Napoli Chenko.

CHAPTER 34

Jamal and Zek cleared customs after waiting an hour for Spanish Melilla officials to search the plane. The government agreed to release the cargo and sent the two men on their way. Jamal unpacked the boxes and reassembled the sniper rifle and the handguns. Zek checked the GPS for lighthouses in Melilla and found two locations.

Zek called Thomas, "We are on the ground and ready to go."

"There will be no negotiations to release Erd. They are going to kill her," said Thomas as he looked out the window. "Be ready for anything. They probably know you're coming. We will land on the water outside the harbor. I'll contact you. Good luck!"

"Copy that." Zek terminated the call, inserted the clip in his gun, and motioned for Jamal to get in the van.

* * * * *

Stark was concerned about Napoli. They had hatched a plan to steal the dagger from their respective organizations. *Napoli was never going to trade for the woman. He was planning to double-cross me all the time. He is a crazy man and will get me killed. Who is he working for, really? Any minute the police will show up at the lighthouse. It's time to move*, thought Stark.

"We are leaving now," ordered Stark. "Tie up the women and put them in the boat. Gather up everything and burn it. Leave nothing for them to follow. Move, move…now!"

The men bound Erd and Kaiya together and placed them below deck in the forward cabin of the large, luxury, power cruiser yacht. Stark left a few men behind to clean up the lighthouse while he made his escape. The sleek boat raced across the water to Spain with its passengers. Stark's master plan was falling apart. Stark thought, *Lofton will decide the next step.*

* * * * *

The GPS took Jamal and Zek to the first lighthouse. The compact van approached the structure, going up the hill on an access road that led to the building. Jamal looked through his binoculars, checking for any signs of activity. Three bullets hit the van, shattering the windshield. Zek steered the vehicle off the road, but a bullet hit a tire, causing the van to roll over on its side.

"Are you hit?" Jamal yelled.

"No, but my leg is trapped. I can't move," responded Zek as he strained in pain while trying to move his leg.

Four more bullets zipped through the van. "We can't stay here. We are sitting ducks," screamed Jamal.

"You go. If you try to get me out, they will kill both of us from this position," said Zek. He continued to try to free his leg.

Jamal crawled down the hill with the Russian-made sniper rifle. Zek fired his pistol at the lighthouse tower to cover Jamal. "I see him," yelled Jamal. He adjusted the rifle sight for his target and fired. "Missed! Damn it!"

"Jamal, squeeze the trigger slowly. Breathe through your shot," shouted Zek.

Four more shots zipped through the van. The smell of gasoline was strong. The gas tank had been hit, and gasoline leaked under the van where Zek was trapped.

"Okay, okay I got this," said Jamal, thinking of the bullet in the shoulder he had taken earlier. He fired again, the bullet hit the sniper; his body slumped over the side of the lighthouse tower and tumbled to the rocks below.

At the van, the gasoline ignited. Smoke and flames were visible under the hood. Zek was coughing and struggling to free his foot. Suddenly, the gas tank exploded. The heat pushed Jamal back. He thought Zek was gone.

Jamal became enraged. He charged toward the lighthouse, running through the brush up the hill. He kicked the door open and bullets flew past his head but he did not stop. He killed one man with his gun and used his fists on the other. When Jamal finished, the man's head was not recognizable. Jamal was covered with blood. He forgot all about Erd and the mission.

After a few minutes, Jamal regained his composure. He splashed water on his face and looked in the mirror. When he turned around, there was Zek standing in the doorway.

"I thought you were—"

"It will take more than a few flames to take me out." Zek grinned as he removed his charred jacket, which was still smoking from the fire.

Jamal hugged Zek. They checked each room for Erd. Jamal said, "They escaped. This was too easy. They've taken her away."

Zek called Thomas. "They left a few men behind but took Erd with them. Nobody is talking here."

"Give me your location. Stay there. Wait for us. We are landing in the harbor," responded Thomas. He was worried about Erd.

"No," said Jamal. "The police will be all over this place soon. We will gather the papers and come to you."

* * * * *

Kaiya's phone call to Dr. McLeay was eventually turned over to the CIA. Within a few hours, the agency had triangulated where the call originated in Melilla. Agents were scrambled to the location to find the missing JPL scientist.

The van explosion created a huge plume of smoke that was seen for miles. The CIA agent in command of the rushed mission was JB Sutton. His plane had been delayed in Casablanca, and he pulled the short straw to lead the investigation of Kaiya's cell phone message.

JB drove past the smoldering van. He noticed the bullet holes and thought, *Someone had a party here.*

At the lighthouse, he found three dead bodies and weapons, but no JPL scientist. He called in the details to Langley. JB requested satellite pictures of the location from the past three hours. He hoped to find images to lead him to the missing person. One picture, taken two hours before he arrived, got his attention. He muttered to himself, "Miss Erd, what are you doing here?" He could not instantly identify the others, but he later confirmed Kaiya's identity from the photo of two women handcuffed together.

Local police sirens wailed in the background, approaching from the west. JB hurriedly took a few pictures and left the lighthouse before the police arrived. JB sent a text message to Jack. "We need to talk. Your girl Miss Erd is captive with someone I'm tracking. Call me." The message was sent to the number Jack gave him when they met by chance in the Casablanca Airport a few days earlier.

CHAPTER 35

Black smoke billowed from behind the bus when it came to a stop in Nashville. Dawson was the last to exit. To his surprise, Pete was standing at the gate with two men dressed in black. Dawson hugged Pete. "I thought you were—"

"Dead? Yeah, for a minute I thought so too. These guys picked me up six weeks ago. They don't talk much. I got a second chance when I agreed to be trained to be part of the Obsidian Order. It's not bad. I get to carry a gun, learn about martial arts, knives, and poisons. Believe it or not, I like it. I'm actually pretty good. See, I lost twenty pounds," Pete said, flexing his new muscles. He pointed the way to the car.

"Where are we going?" asked Dawson.

"To an uninhabited island in the Bahamas. Believe me, it's no resort. The Obsidians train there. It's safe."

"But why take me there?"

"Just following orders," answered Pete. He pointed to the leader of the extraction team. He continued, "Do you need help with that bag?"

"No. No I got it." Dawson responded nervously as he hurriedly grabbed the bag and walked with the three men to the vehicle. Dawson felt a little safer seeing Pete with the Obsidians. However, their reputation as assassins made him uneasy.

Safely in the air in a small jet flying over the Smokey Mountains, Dawson breathed a sigh of relief. He thought about Dr. Easton's death and the mysterious new machine in the gym bag in the seat next to him. He closed his eyes and slipped into a deep sleep.

The plane landed with no incident on a private landing strip in the Bahamas. Dawson struggled to wake up. He hoped the last twenty-four hours had been a dream or, better yet, a nightmare that he would soon forget. The leader of the Obsidians was standing over him when Dawson's eyes opened. Now he knew he was not dreaming.

The man said, "My name is Ragi." He extended his hand and pulled Dawson out of his seat. He continued, "We need to leave for Spain in a few hours after we refuel."

"What? I can't go. I've got work to do. I got—"

"Bro, we need to go. Wheels up in ninety minutes," said Pete. He handed Dawson the phone. "It's Thomas."

"Dawson, the machine works, right?"

"Yes, but I need to work out some bugs. I need a few days to study—"

"Dawson, we do not have time to study. Do what you can now and during the flight. We will need to use the machine to save Erd," Thomas responded.

"Thomas, this thing could kill us all."

"You're our only option." Then the phone went silent.

Dawson's eyes grew large as he looked at Pete. "Hey, I need somewhere to work on this thing. Can you help me?"

"No problem, let's go to the hangar. We got all kinds of tools and stuff in there. Don't worry, we can do this," said Pete. The two men walked slowly into the hanger.

* * * * *

The European space agency followed occurrences of seismic waves in the United States with great interest. Experts from CERN were called in to determine if wormhole activity was involved. A different occurrence was reported weeks earlier, emanating from stretches of the Sahara Desert near the Moroccan border. An investigation was launched. The report noted a small village where the population had vanished without a trace. The report concluded that the village had been relocated, but there was no confirmation from the government of where they'd gone. At the time, there appeared to be no apparent threat from terrorists. No one sent an alarm to NATO, until the report was filed. In response to the new inquiry, the British sent agents from MI6 to find the missing villagers and determine who was responsible.

News of a possible new weapon spread through informal channels. European intelligence agencies sent agents to the United States to snoop around NASA and DC to learn more about the terrorist attack at the New Jersey farmhouse and the mysterious disappearance of a JPL scientist. Washington quietly detained two soldiers for leaking information to a cable news network about an alien weapon found at the New Jersey dairy farm. The news story was quashed, but the whispers continued.

At the White House, the national security director held a briefing for the task force searching for the source of the terrorist attack on the MIT lab. On the screen behind him was a picture of a blond, blue-eyed man. The director pointed at the screen. "This man is Napoli Chenko, known to the CIA. His code name was Ivan. He was the former undersecretary of the KGB before he left to work security for an oil tycoon until the oligarch was forced to flee the country. Napoli's special skills found him a home in the Russian mafia. Most in the intelligence community think he is still working for the KGB. Napoli's reputation for having a deadly flash temper is legendary. Once, he threatened to kill a general for corruption. The general was later found dead in his swimming pool. The government ruled the death as an accident but the army never believed the report. At the funeral, Napoli showed up smoking a cigar. Days later, the general's entire staff of officers resigned in protest, fearing they might become the next victim of another accident."

The director continued, "Two years ago, rumors of the Russians seeking a new type of weapon spread throughout the intelligence community. Napoli Chenko's name is mentioned most often in connection with international arms espionage. The CIA suspects his ties to Russian mafia are now a cover for his activities involved with acquiring stolen technology for the Russian military. A potential new weapon technology could change the balance of power in favor of Russia. The terrorists killed in New Jersey and Boston all had tattoos that indicate they were soldiers in the Russian mob."

CHAPTER 36

In 1985, an archeologist discovered a burial mound located in southern Spain near Granada. The dig site was littered with hundreds of small white tents, with workers carefully removing dirt to preserve ancient artifacts until the ruins of a medieval castle were discovered. Heavy equipment had removed tons of earth before workmen came upon a mysterious stone formation on the structure. The stone walls appeared to have been reduced to molten rock, crystallized into a porous material. The government quietly closed the site to the public after the discovery of the ancient structure. Local police closed the roads to the remote area. The air space was patrolled by the military until a temporary structure was built to cover the sprawling site.

The permanent structure was an enormous, gray thirty-acre building, five stories in height covering the location of the castle ruins and the grounds. Rumors raged about finding a UFO or ancient dinosaur bones but no formal announcement was ever made about the mysterious location. This region of Spain had not had volcanic activity for thousands of years, yet there was damage to a small portion of the structure. The unexplained event had collapsed a third of the building into a pile of molten rock.

Soon after construction of the cavernous building, a local newspaper reporter bribed his way into the secure facility to take pictures of the partially destroyed castle with hopes of publishing them for the world to see. The reporter's body was later discovered in his car, which was crushed in a deep ravine along the Spanish coast. The police reported his car ran off the road to avoid hitting a deer. The remains of a deer were found near the skid marks of the vehicle. The reporter's camera was not found among the wreckage. Colleagues suspected foul play, but no one dared to speak publicly about their suspicions. No other reporter attempted to penetrate the secrecy of the facility. The warning message to the media was loud and clear. *Enter at your own risk.* The only sign on the electrified fence around the building read: Lofton Industries—No Trespassing. Personal cars were not allowed at the facility. Employees were shuttled in via bus or helicopter to minimize vehicle traffic.

Between the ten-foot fence and the building was a no-man's land with armed patrols. Dogs and high-tech surveillance equipment monitored every movement beyond the walls. The fortifications of the huge complex were sound proofed with reinforced concrete. Built like a fortress, the building was unusually bright inside, with the roof illuminated as if it were day. The ceiling was painted with a blue background and billowing clouds to mimic the sky. A computer controlled the climate and atmosphere. Banister Lofton pulled strings with the Spanish government to take control of the site, under the guise that it was needed to mine for rare-earth elements believed to be located near the ruins. Company representatives persuaded the defense minister that the resource was needed to construct a new-generation weapons system.

Mr. Lofton, now almost eighty, had not left this secret compound for over thirty years. He became obsessed with the dagger and its secrets. News of a dagger found by the

African Brotherhood in Zimbabwe troubled him. Lofton had persuaded Fredrick Eddington to obtain the object with the lure of gold. However, Eddington's fixation on diamonds became his undoing. Through the centuries, the legend of the dagger swirled about campfires in the Sahara Desert where Berber horsemen told stories of the Great Akin and his feats of heroism. His trademark was the dagger he carried with him into battle. Akin and the dagger disappeared more than seven hundred years ago. Lofton did not believe the legend of a great warrior. However, he did believe the dagger contained the secret that caused the damage to the castle. Lofton believed the dagger was from a different time, maybe long ago millenniums in the past or from the future.

Banister knew at his first sight of the partially destroyed castle with its great stones melted into layers of smooth rock that something magical had happened there. In the mysterious laboratory of the ancient castle diagrams of a dagger were scattered on the floor. There were images of its parts, disassembled, with illustrations for a machine. Lofton became convinced of the power contained in the missing dagger. He spent a fortune searching for the secret object. His home was in the ancient castle, where its former master once lived hundreds of years ago. Banister had not aged a day since he moved into the ancient structure. His steely green eyes and six-foot muscular frame were still that of the fifty-year-old overachiever who started the endeavor. Lofton discovered, shortly after he moved into the castle, that the aging process had stopped. His aging accelerated if he was away from the castle for more than forty-eight hours. His bones would ache until he returned to what now had become his prison.

Banister started on his journey before he was born. Lofton's father was the family historian. He often read journals written by his great, great grandfather about the legend of a secret Moorish weapon that disappeared as quickly as it appeared. The details in the elder's diary left much for the imagination and created the lore of a mysterious weapon that could vanquish the Spanish empire. The Lofton family wealth could be traced back to twelfth-century Spain, when a blacksmith developed a sword made of steel stronger than any made during that period. Before long, the blacksmith became the arms maker for the Spanish king and his knights. Word of the new steel swords spread throughout Europe.

Soon after, the unknown blacksmith became wealthy by producing arms for Christian pilgrims headed for the Crusades in the Holy Land. The Crusades were military campaigns authorized by the Roman Catholic Church to fight Muslims to restore Christian access to Jerusalem. Crusades were fought starting in the tenth century and lasted until the fourteenth century. With the help of the pope, Christian pilgrims also joined forces to remove the Muslim Moors from the Iberian Peninsula, current-day Spain. This came to be known as the Spanish Crusades. One of the blacksmith's sons became a Knights Templar during the Spanish Crusades. These crusades resulted in the ultimate defeat of the Moors in Granada in 1492. It was that knight, Banister's ancestor, who had witnessed the mysterious Moorish weapon seven hundred years ago.

Banister retired twenty years ago; however, he was still the chairman of the board of his family's company. Funding for the secret castle project was buried on a long list of company locations under the category of research and development. The company took control of the archeological excavation in the mid-1980s after it became clear that the structure was intentionally buried under tons of earth. The interior was protected from the earthen grave by covering the windows and all points of entry with stone and clay to preserve the secrets for some future time.

Lofton engaged historians to research Spanish and Moorish historical records for clues of why something of the structure's size would be buried under a mountain of dirt and clay, but nothing was found. Banister recognized that it would have required hundreds or thousands of men to haul the earth to cover the structure. *Why not simply destroy it?* thought Banister. Banister became obsessed with the mystery until he discovered the answer to his question. He thought of the nuclear disasters at Chernobyl and Three-Mile Island and then he knew. Something catastrophic had happened there. Something so incredible that it frightened those in power to the extent that they abandoned the castle ruins and covered them up for fear the event could happen again. Banister started to sweat and his hands shook as he thought about the unknown event. He realized that it was not a weapon his family had thought about for centuries, but an experiment that went terribly wrong.

Lofton's scientists and engineers searched for any unstable chemical element that could have caused a stone structure to melt like wax, but they found nothing except small traces of radiation. Then the scientists realized that certain laws of physics did not apply within the ancient castle. The mystery was linked to the unusual stones used to construct the castle, which included a mix of cobalt, uranium, and another unknown material.

The discovery explained the slow aging of Banister and the other scientists who worked in the secret compound. Banister's brain cells regenerated at an alarming rate, he rarely slept, and immortality started him thinking of building his own empire. Voices from the shadows of the ancient castle were now directing his actions. A few of Banister's closest advisers suspected a slight madness had set in, but they were afraid to say anything.

Lofton dreamed of renaming the African continent New Elysium. His new weapon to achieve that goal was developed at the secret castle compound. The weapon caused blood vessels in the brain to disintegrate. The rapid regeneration of his brain cells created a genius in his madness. He discovered a way to enhance the radio-frequency radiation from existing cell towers. Initially, his scientists reported that the new technology would revolutionize the wireless communication industry. It would instantly make Lofton Industries a major player in cellular technology and bring billions of dollars in profits. News reports touted the potential of the technology. Soon orders for the little gray boxes that housed the Lofton processor were coming in from all over the world.

Unknown to everyone, however, Lofton was not interested in making more money or great benefits from faster communications that would result from his discovery. He became fixated on the damage he could cause by manipulating the device to turn it into a new weapon. Researchers warned Lofton that very high levels of radio-frequency radiation could cook human tissue and cause serious harm. Privately, he refined his new device to focus the frequency radiation specifically to damage the brain with a terminal effect. As an added layer to his plan, he hired rogue hackers to write code to spread an electronic virus to mobile phones connected to towers enhanced by the Lofton gray boxes. The enhancement allowed Banister to target his misery and spread terror and panic around the world.

Banister planned to use the weapon to force world governments to clear large areas of land for his new kingdom. Sub-Saharan Africa was his first target. He coveted the natural resources. Eastern Europe was next. He would save North America for his last conquest. South America and other Spanish-speaking countries would be annexed. He needed workers to build his vast new empire. The weapon testing was almost complete. The rest of the world would come around to the new world order.

The weapon was already deployed, hidden on cellular towers in plain sight. The high-tech devices were sold to unsuspecting governments under the guise of improving wireless service and as a surveillance tool to monitor Internet and data traffic. Instead, the twenty-pound gray boxes contained doomsday devices that would change the world forever.

The international intelligence community buzzed about the news of over one thousand people missing from the village in the Sahara Desert and a mysterious terrorist attack in the United States. Rumors of a new weapon technology created a rift between allies until the US ambassador to the United Nations received an ultimatum.

The note read, "Evacuate or perish in twenty-four hours." Included in the note were the GPS coordinates of the village where people had vanished on the Moroccan border six weeks earlier. British intelligence confirmed that fifteen hundred people had disappeared without a trace.

Within hours, news agencies from around the world reported on mysterious deaths in small towns and villages in Africa, Europe, and Asia. The panic spread with many fleeing rural areas for large cities, hoping to avoid the phenomenon. The cryptic message to the United Nations gave no clue of what the unknown threat meant.

* * * * *

Banister Lofton was asleep when the call came from Stark as his boat made a hasty departure from the Melilla lighthouse. Banister's assistant woke him with the news that Stark and his prisoner, Miss Erd, were in the Mediterranean heading toward the Spanish coast. Immediately, Banister ordered his security team to take the helicopter to Malaga harbor to intercept the boat to retrieve the occupants.

Stark failed to mention that he was also bringing Kaiya, the missing JPL scientist. The roar from the yacht's three powerful 480 hp diesel engines was silenced three hours later in the harbor in Malaga, Spain. From the distance, Erd heard the sound of a helicopter approaching. She was blindfolded and could not tell exactly where they were, but she knew they were in Spain. Erd sent that last thought to Thomas before the men drugged her again.

CHAPTER 37

The midnight bullet train from St. Petersburg to Moscow covered four hundred miles in less than four hours. Goode hoped Napoli would not follow him there. In the early morning hours in Moscow, a lone figure waited in the shadows, watching passengers disembark from the train. Goode hailed a taxi for the airport. He needed to leave the country as soon as possible. As the taxi parked to pick up Goode, the stranger approached him with his hand in his pocket. He motioned for Goode to get in the car. Goode's heart pounded. His thoughts raced as he thought about the blue-eyed devil, Napoli, he'd run from in St. Petersburg to escape certain death.

Goode said to the driver in Russian, "Domodedovo International Airport." He looked over at his co-passenger who still had not said a word.

Finally, Goode blurted out, "Are you here for me?" Sweat rolled down his forehead.

"Yes, I have your orders from the elders." The stranger handed Goode an envelope from the pocket where Goode thought he had a gun.

He opened the envelope to find a new passport with new identity papers and airline tickets for Ethiopia, Addis Ababa.

"What's this?"

"It's not safe for you in Ghana, anymore. The Russians will track you there. The elders have a new mission for you. You will learn more when you get there." The stranger asked the taxi driver to stop at the corner. He leaned over to Goode and whispered, "Don't break the chain." Then the man got out of the taxi and walked into the street and down the stairs into the subway.

The taxi drove off, heading for the airport. Relieved that the man was not a mafia hit man, Goode breathed a sigh of relief. At the airport, Goode stopped to text a message to the bank in Switzerland to confirm that the Russian funds had cleared for the diamond transaction. He then continued the dash through the airport for his flight to Berlin and on to Addis Ababa. Goode had had enough of the cold weather and the intrigue dealing with Napoli. Although he was apprehensive about the mysterious mission in Ethiopia, he understood the Russian mafia would not stop until they had control of the diamonds. He was exposed now and needed to disappear. Goode was saddened by the thought of not being able to return to Ghana. He had no choice but to trust the Brotherhood's elders.

Goode was of no value to Napoli since he knew he didn't have the dagger to trade. Napoli could have killed him in the car; instead he let him get away. He liked Goode in his own way. However, he wanted Goode to know he knew where the Brotherhood got their diamonds and that others knew too. To him it was not personal, just business. Once Napoli decided to take out his boss, there was no more need for games. He thought a little fear was good for business.

Stark was in Lofton's helicopter when he got the call from Napoli. "I'm the boss now. Give me the girl."

"No, I am turning the girl over to my people. You will have to deal with them. I'm not going to let you get me killed," whispered Stark before hanging up the phone.

Across from Stark, Banister's burly security chief motioned for Stark's phone and his gun. The security chief kept his hand on his weapon to make sure there was no misunderstanding. He tossed the phone out the door as the helicopter circled over the water. A blindfold was given to Stark. Now, like his prisoners, he was a captive.

* * * * *

The fog cleared enough to land the cargo plane outside of the harbor in Melilla, Spain. The landing on water was a new experience for several of the passengers. Thomas was the most relieved to hear the engine silenced. They sat for a few minutes until the pilot rose from his seat and smiling widely said, "You see, I know these waters. Landing smooth, yes?"

Jack nodded, looked at Thomas, and said, "Yes, every landing is a good landing."

Salman's uncle hurriedly rushed to the back of the plane and started inflating a raft; then he tossed it out of the cargo door. He said, "It's dangerous for the plane to stay here. They have patrols. You must go now!" He pointed toward the shore. "It's only five miles from here."

Thomas and Jack loaded themselves onto the raft. Salman waved good-bye to the men as they floated away from the plane. The turboprop engines fired up, and the roar of the plane soon was heard overhead. Waves from the plane's wake pushed the small raft closer to Melilla Harbor.

Erd's message to Thomas arrived just as the plane landed, and he announced to Jack, "She's alive!" Looking toward the northeast he continued, "We're running out of time."

Jack and Thomas rowed quietly to the harbor in the darkness. The moonless night and splashes from the paddles pushing the water away sent Thomas's mind back to the dream he'd had while recovering from plastic surgery. At the time, he'd thought it was a side effect from the drugs given to him to make him sleep and speed his recovery, but now it was becoming clear that it was actually a vision, a warning of a looming threat from Spain. Thomas sent a message to his command ship, the *Scorpion*, for the estimated time of arrival for the boat to pick them up in the harbor.

Finally, there was a light flashing in code, the same signal over and over again. Jack pointed over to the left at the signal.

"That must be Zek's signal," said Jack. Thirty minutes later, Jamal and Zek were safely on the raft. The four men floated out to sea, waiting for the boat from the *Scorpion*.

After a few minutes, Thomas said, "It is good to see you guys. We must go to Spain to complete our mission."

Nothing else was said. Everyone sat silently, listening to the waves crashing against the raft. The hum of the motor on a small boat could be heard in the distance until the craft cut its engine to dock with the raft. The men departed Melilla Harbor in darkness and headed out to sea for the *Scorpion*. The drone of the boat motor was all that was heard on the zodiac for the twenty-minute ride to the ship. The men sat silently, rocking over the waves, thinking of the daunting task that lay before them. Jack's phone buzzed with a text from his old boss, JB, from the CIA.

Thomas sent a message to his command ship for the captain to be ready to leave for Spain when they arrived. He thought about the coded message on the paper given to him at the hotel in Calais by the mysterious man called Emissary. *It must be a key to finding where they have Erd*, he thought.

CHAPTER 38

Whispers on the street in the village near the secret Lofton research complex grew more ominous after the reporter was found dead. The townsfolk noticed their phones had echoes and clicking noises in them when they spoke. The Internet service crashed so often, many had given up on e-mail and social media communications. Fear had crept into everyone. At night, guards in body armor from the Lofton facility patrolled the streets with automatic rifles. The local police, consisting of two deputies and a constable, never carried weapons and they didn't go out unless they were called. National security was the reason the government allowed a private firm to secure the area around the massive Lofton facility.

Quietly, in the wee hours of the morning, a few men gathered in the basement of a local pub. The Lofton security force had finished their nightly patrol. A patron who had fought in the Spanish Civil War held court at a makeshift bar made of empty beer kegs. He and a few friends drank together most nights to forget about the fear that had overtaken their town.

The old man's speech was slurred from too much wine when he said, "It started when they uncovered that old ruin. That dark evil place had been hidden for over one thousand years and then they started digging with their white coats and pick axes until they woke up the devil himself." The three men sitting on wooden boxes listened while the elderly man pointed in the direction of the

Lofton facility. One man tried to get him to lower his voice, but he would have nothing of it.

The frail man said, "What are they going to do, kill me? I am one step from the grave already. I'm just saying what you know is true in your hearts. There is something evil over there. I felt it as soon as those big cranes dug out that old castle. They buried it for a reason, you know. This is not science or national security. This darkness is casting a shadow over all of us."

"But the governor said the plant will produce technology to keep Spain safe. The security forces are here to protect us," argued his elderly friend.

"You mean mercenaries. And protect us from what? They are listening to our phones and patrolling our streets like we are the enemy," said the old man.

Then there was the sound of footsteps and banging on the basement door. It was the Lofton security force. The sergeant in command yelled through the door, "Sir, there is a report of a disturbance at this location. We need to take you in for questioning."

Moments later, the door was broken into pieces, and the guards dragged the four drunken elderly dissidents from the basement and took them to an undisclosed location. Their names were added to a list of ninety other people who had mysteriously disappeared since the castle ruins had been unearthed. In the nearby village, fear ruled the day, and the whispers were hushed into an eerie silence.

* * * * *

The castle ruins that were unearthed thirty years ago did release something else. Banister Lofton changed after spending weeks on the site inspecting the near-pristine condition of the interior rooms of the structure. The clay seals on the doors and other openings were almost perfect in preventing air and moisture from decaying the building and its contents. The armory was filled with a perfectly preserved collection of priceless weapons dating back to the Roman Empire. Lofton found a silk robe worn by the master of the castle. He wore it occasionally, imagining himself living there and ruling his kingdom. Unknown to Banister, long-dormant, tiny, parasitic wormlike creatures lost in the thick dust of the forbidden castle entered his ears and infected his brain.

That led to the beginning of his obsession with the castle. He supervised every detail of restoring everything authentic to the period of 1000 AD. Lofton had every room, from the feasting hall to the armory, redone. Since he was an arms merchant, the armory was his favorite room. Banister's collection of swords from Caesar's Rome covered the wall as a centerpiece. He organized the room according to the time period. Lofton added the family's prized collection of swords and daggers forged in his ancestor's blacksmith shop. Those objects were placed in glass cases mounted in the wall with lights to highlight the workmanship. On the opposite wall were muskets, rifles, and handguns that marked his family's transition into the current-day multinational arms manufacturer. Ancient body armor and shields accented the corners of the room. Millions of euros were spent meticulously recreating the palace housed inside a concrete fortress.

* * * * *

The helicopter landed as the sun slowly rose in the east. Erd and Kaiya were awake, but their heads were covered with hoods. The two women were carried from the helipad located on top of the massive Lofton complex to an elevator that quickly transported them to the main floor of the facility. The huge doors closing behind them pounded shut. The golf cart they rode in cleared the various security sections in the enormous facility. Miss Erd heard sounds of men marching in formation and the click of automatic weapons at each sentry point. She feared for the Brotherhood if they attempted to rescue her. Erd started crying when she thought of Thomas being killed. Soon her thoughts went to him. "Do not come for me. There is only death here. Stay away." Then at the last checkpoint, the electronic signal blocking technology was activated. Erd felt her connection to Thomas terminate.

"We know all about your African Brotherhood," a voice announced as the women were secured in a tiny room in the castle. The ancient building was located in the remote southeast corner of the sprawling facility.

"Did you get a message out to your friends?" said the security chief as he closed a steel-plated door. The electronic lock clicked from green to red. He left the two women in darkness. "Now we wait," he said, looking at Stark. Erd read Stark's thoughts. She discovered Stark had a flash drive in his pocket that contained a recording of his torture of her.

Inside the control center of the Lofton compound, radar and satellite surveillance monitors beamed images of the Mediterranean and the Spanish coastline as they searched for potential threats. Drones and unmanned aerial vehicles armed with missiles to stop any vessel were flown along the coast. A fishing trawler flying a Turkish flag went unnoticed by drones flying overhead.

Hours passed while Erd and Kaiya wrestled to remove the hoods from their heads and the duct tape from their mouths. Finally, Erd could speak to her cellmate without linking her thoughts with the stranger. Erd said, "We must get out of here. They are setting a trap for my people who are trying to rescue us."

Erd used her teeth to free Kaiya's hands. Then she felt the locking mechanism of the door. The flashing red light was the only light in the room. After a few minutes, Erd asked, "Do you have any ideas? Aren't you a scientist or something?"

Kaiya was dazed and her mind was numb from being drugged and beaten by Stark while she was at the lighthouse. Her mind shut down, and she sat in the corner rocking back and forth with her eyes closed.

Erd grabbed her shoulders and stood her up. "Look, sister, it's you and me. That's it. Snap out of it. We have to do this on our own."

Kaiya looked into Erd's eyes. "Give me a minute." She rubbed her eyes and started walking around the small room. "Let me think. Let me think." She started patting her jeans pockets and found a small black box the size of a cell phone.

"What is that? Is it a phone?"

"No, it's an experimental electronic device designed to measure electromagnetic waves. I may be able to adjust the battery polarization to open the lock." Using a hairpin, Kaiya sat in a corner in the dark and worked with the small device. Suddenly, *click, click*—the light turned green. The huge metal door opened.

Miss Erd hugged Kaiya, took her hand, and led the way out of the room. In a whisper, she said, "We need to get as far from here as possible. Let's find a place to hide until my people can find us."

"Who are your people? Are you with the terrorists?" asked Kaiya, as she locked the door behind them, which turned the light on the lock back to red.

"Terrorists? Seriously, I doubt we would have been tied up together if that were the case," Erd said with a frown.

"No, it's better that you not ask any more questions. Let's focus on getting out of here," continued Erd. The women ran across the hall into a large formal dining room.

They quickly hid in a closet and locked the door behind them. A few minutes later, footsteps echoed in the hall. A guard checked the cell doors to confirm they were locked. For the first time in forty-eight hours, Erd felt alive again and in control of her destiny, even though she was running for her life. Her thoughts went out to Thomas, even though she didn't know if he could hear them.

Erd's mind raced as she thought about Stark and the flash drive full of secrets stolen from her. She knew what she needed to do. Her mind was clear. Erd left Kaiya in the closet while she stalked her prey.

CHAPTER 39

The White House Security Council meeting lasted six hours. It ended with no solution to curb the rash of deaths that had caused entire communities to vanish in fear. The body count was up to six thousand in five African countries, and the number of people fleeing the countryside had risen to twenty thousand. The CIA was tasked with finding the source of the terror threat. Several eastern European countries reported similar anomalies. Fear spread worldwide. People in small rural farming communities were now fleeing to the big cities. Roads in Kenya, Poland, Nigeria, Estonia, and the Congo were clogged with women and children.

On board the *Scorpion*, Thomas had left the coded message given to him by the stranger in Calais with an analyst in the control center. The message included a GPS location for a research facility in Spain, near Granada. The analyst prepared a profile of the plant with background information on the CEO, Banister Lofton. When Thomas and the rest of the men gathered for an assessment of the situation, it became clear that they could not launch an assault on a secure facility with government protection.

Thomas motioned to Jack, "Use this signal scrambler on this phone and call your friend JB. See what he knows about Erd and this facility."

"Why would they take Erd there?" Jack responded. "There must be something else working here. This is no kidnapping. This is something else."

"Yeah, we need another approach. Dawson may be our only option," Thomas said. He looked over at Jamal and Zek as they prepared their weapons.

"Hey, we are going after her, right?" Jamal stood up with his hands extended. He pointed his finger into Thomas's chest.

"Yes, but we need to consider the best way. Look at this facility. It is a military compound. Although this ship is equipped with some capabilities, we can't launch an attack from here. They would blow us out of the water." Thomas pointed toward the NATO airbase twenty miles away. The fortified fence and watchtowers on the perimeter were shown on the satellite photo.

"The main building is huge," responded Jamal. "You could fit four football fields in that thing and have room for a practice field, too. What is this place?" Jamal commented while checking the radio headsets they would wear on the mission to free Erd.

"Hey man, I don't speak any Spanish, but this will do my talking," Jamal said, holding a .357 magnum in his hand.

"Do you speak any languages?" responded Zek.

"Yeah, I speak crazy. Now ask me something else," said Jamal in a low tone.

"Okay, but we can't take that cannon with us. We need to use a silencer. That gun will call out the entire army on us." Zek laughed as he handed Jamal a 9mm automatic with a silencer.

Jack went topside to contact JB. The phone rang several times with no answer. Jack paced the deck of the ship saying, "Answer the phone."

On the third attempt, JB answered. "Speak to me."

"It's Jack. I got your text."

"Oh yeah, well, good, at least something works around here," responded JB as he looked at the monitor on his laptop. "No time for small talk. I've got a missing woman —a JPL scientist—and from the looks of things, she was tied up with your Miss Erd at the lighthouse in Melilla before the fireworks started."

"Missing scientist. Really?" asked Jack

"Yeah. The crazy thing is there is some weird science going on here. We can't figure out how she got from Vernon, New Jersey, to Morocco in less than two hours. You got any ideas?" JB asked while tapping the keys on his laptop.

Jack got quiet. He didn't respond.

"Look, they're climbing up my butt for this missing person. Work with me. What are we dealing with here? I know they got your girl too?"

"Right. Yes, Miss Erd was kidnapped about forty-eight hours ago. I don't know about the other woman. We narrowed our search for Erd to a weapons research facility located near Granada, Spain. Lofton Laboratories," responded Jack.

"What? Oh shit," said JB.

"Do you know anything about this location?"

"It's the black hole. It's a super-secret facility. The national government gave a private contractor control over fifty square miles, including the local civilian population. They will not tell us what they're working on. We sent a few contractors over there to poke around for us. Both were killed in a freak car accident. It was not enough to start an international incident, but we got the message," said JB.

"Why would the government give a private company that much control?" asked Jack.

"Well, for one thing, you are talking about Banister Lofton, who is only the fourth richest person on the planet, if you believe the money counters. He owns millions of acres of land in Spain. His weapons systems are purchased by the who's who of nations, even the Russians. Banister Lofton is not a lightweight. I am sure if he asked for it he got it. The rumor is he is getting senile. He's a recluse. No one has seen him in over forty years. He sends his henchman out to do his bidding," responded JB as he paced the floor.

"This is not good," said Jack.

"Hey, there is lot of concern on my end about a new weapon being developed in the States. Our scientist disappeared while investigating the site in New Jersey. Our folks are getting pretty worked up about it. We've got dead bodies in New Jersey and in Cambridge, a few dead Russians, too," said JB.

"Russians? Can you work with me to get Erd and your scientist out of the Lofton facility?" responded Jack.

"Officially, I am on temporary assignment to track down the missing scientist. That's it. The heavy weights are flying in tomorrow. I don't think you want to deal with them. You are still on the CIA's watch list for questioning on that matter in South Africa a few months ago. Call me in a few hours. I'll see what I can do," JB responded.

"Thanks, we need to act soon." Jack terminated the call.

* * * * *

Dawson exited the plane in Granada, Spain. He'd completed the modifications to the helmet from the notes left by Dr. Easton. Pete flanked Dawson as they walked on the tarmac to the rental vehicle. A customs agent stopped Dawson for a random inspection. He emptied his carry-on bag of the tools he'd brought on board and the helmet. Dawson hands began to sweat as he watched the customs agent handle the device.

If he makes one wrong move, the lights will start flashing and someone may disappear, he thought. The customs agent put the helmet on his head to see if it worked as a game console, according to Dawson's description. The helmet was too small. The agent handed it back to him and let his party depart the airport.

Thomas, Jack, Jamal, and Zek took the boat to shore in El Varadero, Spain. The *Scorpion* moved out to sea into international waters. An hour later, Dawson met up with the rest of the Brotherhood in an abandoned farmhouse on the highway leading to Granada.

After a brief moment for everyone to greet Dawson and Pete, Thomas pulled Dawson aside. He said, "We think they're holding Erd thirty miles from here in a secure facility. I sent for you because there is no way to get in unless we use the machine. Can you control the destination? How many can travel with you?"

Uneasy, Dawson responded by looking at the bag that contained the helmet. "Look, I've only used it once. The brain wave interface is tricky. It was pretty scary to see my body parts dissolve into thin air. I've made some changes that will allow the use of GPS coordinates. I think those modifications will prevent materialization into other objects, like a steel beam or a wall. That would be ugly. Nothing has been tested. I need more time."

"Will it work?" demanded Thomas. He stared straight into Dawson's eyes.

"I don't know, Thomas. I don't understand why it works at all. This is crazy science." Dawson's hands started to shake uncontrollably.

Thomas put his arm around Dawson's shoulder and said, "Brother, it's alright. Sorry I pressed you. I know this has been difficult, but you are our only option to save Erd."

"Everything is happening so fast. I saw them blow Dr. Easton's brain apart. The image is still fresh in my mind. Who are these people chasing me?" asked Dawson.

"Russians. They're after the machine and our diamonds. They kidnapped Erd to trade her for the dagger. When they realized you had succeeded with developing the machine, they cut off negotiations for Erd. That's all we know. We suspect they're holding her in a facility over the ridge," said Thomas. He pointed at a map of the location on his tablet computer. He gave Dawson the GPS coordinates.

"We lost three of our men in New Jersey at the lab, too," responded Dawson.

"Yeah, I know. We are taking a beating. Can we do this?"

"Give me a few minutes. I need to run a few calculations before I can answer your question." Dawson took Thomas's tablet computer and his tool bag over to a table near the window.

CHAPTER 40

In the castle, on the monitor, a silent alarm signaled an infrared signature moving slowly in a vent shaft above the long hallway near the cell where Erd and Kaiya had been held captive. Stark was alone in the control room when the alarm went off. Stark walked to the cell door to check the occupants. He discovered they had escaped. He did not alert Lofton's men. Instead, he grabbed a knife from the holster to follow the vent above.

Stark watched as Erd opened the cover to slip down to the floor. From behind, Stark grabbed Erd's hair and placed his knife under her throat. He said, "Prepare to meet your maker."

Believing she would be killed, Erd screamed out to Thomas in her mind. Stark was dragging her backward toward the cell door when suddenly the blade of a sword penetrated his chest. Blood squirted out from the curved steel protruding from his chest. He fell backward and his body wiggled until his eyes went cold.

Kaiya let go of the sword when Stark fell to the ground. She rushed to Erd to see if she was okay. Erd was shocked to see Kaiya.

"Is he dead?" asked Erd.

"Yes," responded Kaiya. She coldly pulled the sword from his back, then wiped the blood from the blade. "Help me move his body before the guards come back."

Erd got his feet while Kaiya pulled his arms. Kaiya opened the metal door and the women dragged Stark's body inside. Erd took off his shirt and wiped the blood from the floor. They heard footsteps approach.

"Quick, get back inside. We will lock ourselves in the cell. They are looking for us," said Erd.

Erd and Kaiya bound each other's hands and sat on top of Stark's body in case the guards looked through the window to check. Two guards stood outside the door for twenty minutes. One guard opened the door, using a flashlight to confirm the prisoners were still inside, while the other one inspected the open vent down the hall. The light flashed on the two women's faces. Then the guard closed the door and locked it. The light turned red again.

"What was that with you and the sword?" asked Erd.

"He deserved it. He was a pig," said Kaiya. She pulled the sword from under his body. "I did competitive fencing in college. I almost went to the Olympics when I was a sophomore, but I had to give it up. Look at the craftsmanship of this blade. Incredible."

Erd just looked at Kaiya for a few moments then said, "Well, okay then, pick me out one of those things when we get out of here. You made quick work of this bastard. He deserved every bit of that. I didn't see that one coming." Erd retrieved the flash drive from his shirt pocket.

The castle was on full alert. Flashing red lights in the hallway were aglow. Security teams were searching for Stark. Banister ordered a guard to be posted outside of Miss Erd's cell door. Kaiya peeked through the glass as she stood on Stark's body. She confirmed their worst fear: the guard had not left.

"We need to make a break soon before more security comes," said Kaiya. "I only see one guard."

"Can you take him?" asked Erd as she removed a radio from Stark's pocket in preparation to make a run for it.

"Yes, but I need to divert his attention. When I click the door open, scream to lure him in," instructed Kaiya as she readied herself with the sword.

"Let's do this," said Erd.

The light flashed to green and the door opened.

CHAPTER 41

Banister's little gray boxes, which were installed on cell towers throughout Africa and Eastern Europe, seemed harmless enough. The huge cell towers stood like guardians along highways and meadows everywhere. In the cities, they were hidden on the tops of buildings and on electric poles, too. Cell sites had become so common, people did not even notice them anymore. The technology's presence was welcomed by most, because it represented progress. More bars on mobile phones meant better signal strength. It was an easy sell for Lofton Industries to add its little gray boxes to improve the wireless network performance and help fight the war on terror. Fledgling democracies were looking for new ways to control the Internet and communications to prevent a terrorist attack. Even first-world countries let Lofton add its little boxes on cell tower sites, as they thought enhanced service and more security was needed.

Unfortunately, a madman had control of the Lofton facility that manufactured the gray boxes. In addition to including the circuitry to monitor and enhance web traffic, he had added a weapon that he hoped to use to rule the world. The boxes were systematically installed over a period of a year. Banister pressed the button six weeks ago to test the effectiveness of the device in the Moroccan desert near a remote village. Moments later, a red light blinked and a high-pitched sound was transmitted to all mobile phones. By the end of the day, almost everyone was dead. Those who were not killed, fled, fearing a new plague had struck the village.

Bodies littered the street. Blood flowed from the ear canals of the victims. Banister's new weapon caused massive brain aneurisms. Madness had fully taken over him. Lofton sent in a convoy of trucks under the cover of darkness to collect and dispose of the bodies. He didn't want his secret weapon to be known too soon. The button to arm all of the gray boxes in Africa and Eastern Europe was on his smart wristwatch, connected to his control center.

Napoli Chenko, the new head of the Penquse crime family, cut a deal with Banister Lofton in exchange for control of certain parts of Eastern Europe. He knew Banister was insane, but it didn't matter. He saw the video of the test site in the desert. It was very effective. Banister had created the world's first deadly electronic virus transmitted through any cell tower or mobile device. Who else but a mad man could think of such a creative weapon? Besides, people had called Napoli mad too.

Banister pressed the button on his watch, then turned on the world news channel to see the results of his handy work. Reports of a new plague striking rural communities in Eastern Europe created fear that spread, causing people to flee with their mobile phones, without knowing they were carrying the plague in their pockets. Another ransom note was sent to the United Nations with a demand to clear land and remove governments voluntarily or more would die.

* * * * *

Jack's phone rang. "It's JB. I've got something for you. The facility you mentioned is the right place. It's enormous, but the location you need to focus on is a castle hidden inside. I know this sounds crazy, but this Lofton guy, Banister, restored an ancient castle. He built his research facility around it. Get this: he lives in the castle. However, this is not why I called you. We are getting reports of deaths connected to a threat delivered to the UN two days ago. I know you are trying to save your friend Erd, but we suspect this Banister is behind a new plague in parts of Africa and Eastern Europe. We are hours away from a world panic. People are fleeing rural areas and flooding into the cities. If something happens in the cities, this could be catastrophic."

"JB, what do you want from me? I don't know anything about a plague," responded Jack.

"Look, we can't get to Banister. That place is locked down. If he knew we were onto him, he might do what he has threatened to do," responded JB.

"What are you saying?"

"Your African friends have some unique special abilities. Considering how our scientist was mysteriously transported to Morocco, I think you might be able to get in the castle easier than our guys. I'm just saying. I will text you the coordinates of the castle. You need to take down Banister when you go in to save your friend," said JB as he read from his laptop.

"Is this an official request?" asked Jack

"No. You know how this works. This conversation never took place. We can't acknowledge a rogue African intelligence organization. You guys don't exist. Remember? If you go in, take down Banister," said JB.

"Are you asking for a favor?"

"Just get it done, Jack. We don't do this work looking for medals." JB ignored Jack's question.

"Send the text. If you see me again you owe me big time." Jack terminated the call and dreaded going back inside to tell Thomas what they needed to do.

Jack's phone rang again. "It's JB," said frantically. "We got new reports of thousands of deaths in the US. Hurry! Lofton is using mobile phone networks to kill. The government ordered all world wireless networks to shut down. The systems have been hijacked. Time is running out!"

* * * * *

A black-suited security officer ordered Erd to face the door. Behind the door, Kaiya was hiding. She made a thrust at the man's back, but the body armor blunted the blow. He turned around and lunged at her with his knife, forcing her to the floor. Again, he lunged, grabbing the blade. Kaiya spun her body, flipping over him, and with a slashing motion, sliced his neck above the body armor. He died instantly. Erd was amazed at Kaiya. The scientist cleaned her sword and returned it to the sheath. Erd thought, *We could use someone like her in the Brotherhood. She's smart and deadly.*

Erd said, "You move like a ninja warrior with that thing. After this is over, we should talk."

"You really think we will get out of this alive? This sword is no match for bullets," responded Kaiya as they ran down the hall.

"Don't worry. We just need to stay alive. The brothers are coming. I feel it."

"We need to get out of this castle. If we can make it to the outside, we will have a better chance," Kaiya said as she inspected the huge door at the entrance. "It has the same electronics as the cell door." She removed her hairpin and went to work with her device. Her long black hair fell down the length of her back. They could hear a large group of men running through the corridor toward them. Erd knew time was running out. She sent her thoughts to Thomas.

CHAPTER 42

The World Health Organization doctors examined the bodies recovered from Africa and Eastern Europe. Blood had flooded the brains of the victims. The cause of death in all victims was a massive brain aneurism. The bodies appeared healthy otherwise, no infections or viruses. The victims had nothing in common other than being dead from a brain condition. One researcher noticed that all the victims had mobile phones, but quickly dismissed the link to the cause of death. Although there had been studies conducted on the effects of cell phones on the brain, with a possible link to tumors and cancer, nothing conclusive was found.

Unfortunately, the world was not prepared for Banister Lofton's madness. His immense wealth gave him unfettered access to research on the brain. The parasites that had infected him ate away at his mind, leaving nothing to counter balance primal evil thoughts. He fired anyone who challenged him. Banister secretly arranged for the deaths of the scientists and anyone else involved with the development of his new weapon. Once the gray boxes were deployed, the number of those in his inner circle was reduced even more. Now only he knew what was actually in the cell tower sites upgraded by Lofton Industries.

Banister heard voices in the castle and he imagined himself ruling the world. Banister was now ready to impose his will on the world. He pressed the button on his wristwatch again and turned on the world news to see his work. The UN had missed his deadline to clear the land for his new kingdom. The panic had now spread to the cities. Fear of a new plague filled global news networks.

* * * * *

Dawson completed his calculations. The brothers gathered to hear his assessment. "I can only take one person with me. The number that can travel is limited, based on weight. The wormhole will collapse in sixty seconds after I vanish, which means only two more can follow because of the energy drain on the power source."

"That means only four of us can go on this mission. Who is going to follow Dawson and me?" said Jamal as he checked his gun and ammunition.

"Jamal. Jack and I are going. You need to stay here," commanded Thomas.

"Naw, you got it twisted. I'm head of security. I go first. If you get killed, what happens to our organization? I go first to make sure it is safe for you to follow. That's how it's going to work," demanded Jamal.

The brothers looked at Jamal and Thomas, wondering what would happen. "Look, we don't have time to debate this, Jamal," insisted Thomas.

"This is my job, Thomas. It isn't personal. Let me do it," said Jamal.

Thomas knew Jamal was right. He was thinking of saving Erd, not his obligation to the Brotherhood. Thomas stepped back and nodded. "It's going to be Jamal and Dawson first and then Jack and I will follow. Zek and Pete stay here to monitor communications with the *Scorpion* in case we need support to escape from the facility. Gather your weapons; we go in five minutes."

Jack asked Dawson, "Where's the dagger?"

"I think it's in my backpack. Why do you need it?"

"I need to take it with me," replied Jack.

"I promised Erd I would keep it safe," said Dawson, hesitating while he searched for the object. "I've been through a lot with this thing. I lost an old friend and almost died myself."

"Yeah, I know it's been tough. Trust me. I have a history with the dagger, too. I need to take it into battle," said Jack.

Reluctantly, Dawson handed Jack the dagger. He said, "Do you know how to use it?" Dawson thought about the one-eyed artifact expert who had shown him how to make thrusts with the weapon.

"Yeah, I got it," said Jack. He put the dagger in his belt.

Thomas gathered the men around as Dawson powered up the helmet for the trip into the castle. He raised his hand for all the men to join him in the middle.

Thomas said, "If we die, we die. Let's rid the world of this evil and rescue our sister Erd! Long live the Brotherhood!"

All the men cheered and embraced; then they stepped back to watch in amazement as Dawson and Jamal vanished. Jack nervously stepped over to the place where they had departed and disappeared. Thomas followed.

The brothers stepped forward into the unknown. Maybe it was faith or just hope that things would work out. Regardless of the reason, they did it. Jamal and Dawson passed through the wormhole and appeared in the castle facing ten guards with weapons drawn on Erd and the woman known as Kaiya. The sudden appearance of two men startled everyone. Several men dropped their weapons. Others froze, thinking their eyes had failed them. Finally, the sound of Jamal's weapon striking the remaining men shocked everyone.

Within minutes, Thomas and Jack appeared from the dust. The bright light had faded, and the sound of automatic weapon fire had subsided. The feeling that resulted from walking into the wormhole had disturbed both Thomas and Jack. A few men lay dead before them, with the remainder still in shock. The rest of the men retreated from view.

Dawson ran over to Erd and Kaiya. He pressed the Go sequence buttons on his helmet and said, "Stand close to me." The LED lights flashed on the helmet visor and a beam radiated over the two women. Moments later, they were gone, transported back to the farmhouse with Pete and Zek.

After a few minutes, a second wave of security forces approached from the facility outside. The huge castle door opened, and the men commenced firing their weapons at Jack and Thomas.

Jamal waved at Thomas. He jammed another clip in his weapon and fired into the hall as he shouted at Thomas, "Come on, let's go!"

Thomas knew what to do. He slung the rocket-propelled-grenade launcher on his shoulder and fired at the door. *Boom, boom.* The blast blew the huge doors off their hinges and onto the floor, trapping bodies underneath. The fight was on. Thomas motioned for Jack to go while he and Jamal gave him covering fire.

Jack made his way back into the corridor deeper into the castle, looking for Banister Lofton. Thinking of JB's message that thousands were dying, Jack knew he needed to find Lofton to end the massacre. Jack crawled past the armory to the control room. The collection of swords seemed eerily familiar to him. He had been there before, he thought. Maybe it was a flash back from Akin. Jack pressed a panel on the floor of the control room doorframe. He discovered a secret passage that led below the floor into a huge room lit with candles. The air smelled of a thick musky odor. Jack waited in the shadows until he heard someone talking. The man wore an old silk robe and had long gray hair and a beard.

Banister Lofton said, "Now they will know my rage." He pressed a button on his wristwatch, then said, "Die in fear." He laughed wildly as he spoke to the wall. The room suddenly went dark.

Jack said, "This must be the mad man JB sent me after." He heard men running with automatic weapons outside the door. He reached in his belt for the dagger. On his knees, Jack crawled under a table to get closer to the mad man. The smell turned his stomach, the closer he got. He stood to drive the dagger into Banister, only to discover he was stalking something else. Banister had fled the room, leaving Jack to fight his pet, a two hundred-pound pit bull. The huge dog attacked Jack instantly. The two tumbled until finally the dagger was lodged into the monster's throat. Exhausted, Jack retrieved the dagger and rolled over on the floor, under the bed. Banister entered the room wearing chain mail armor, ready for battle. He saw his dog was dead on the floor in a pool of blood and called out to the intruder to face him in battle.

"Only cowards kill dogs in the dark. Come meet the king in the light," Banister shouted, holding his sword in front of him.

Jack threw down his gun and pulled out his dagger. He reached to his left and pulled on the light switch to show himself. "On guard, you bastard! Tonight you will die!"

The battle ensued with both men striking bloody blows to the head and chest. Jack had never fought with a dagger before, but he fought with skill, making thrusts until his opponent had to retreat.

Jack noticed the watch on Banister's hand and the blinking red light. He thought, *Enough of this, people are dying.* He reached to the floor to retrieve his gun. Jack looked away for a moment, and Banister slashed his chest open. Blood sprayed freely from Jack's body, weakening him.

Banister's eyes enjoyed the sight of his opponent's blood. He stopped to rub his hand in the puddle to taste his prize, and then Jack lunged at Banister, striking his arm and severing his hand in the process. The watch fell to the floor, crashing into many pieces. Jack thrust the dagger into the madman's heart. Banister fell dead.

Jack staggered out of the king's chamber and back to the control room he'd passed earlier. He found a world map on the huge monitor with green dots blinking. He thought, *This must be what JB was talking about.* Jack set several explosive charges of C4 in the control room and then ran out to the corridor to join Thomas and Jamal in the fight. The blast knocked Jack off his feet. The ancient castle walls that had stood for over one thousand years started to collapse. Dust filled the structure. The shooting stopped. Lofton's men fled outside as the ceiling broke away. Thomas dragged Jack's body from under the debris and out of the castle.

The little gray boxes scattered around the world went dark. Their master, Banister Lofton, was dead. Africa and the world were free of the deadly plague.

When Jack woke up, Jamal was standing over him. Jack said, "Don't just stand there, help a brother up."

"We thought you were gone. We patched up your wounds, but you were knocked out," said Jamal.

"You can't kill the Great Akin," Jack said with a smile then looked over at Thomas.

"Who's the Great Akin?" asked Dawson. He powered up the machine to take Jamal and himself back to the farmhouse.

Thomas laughed. "It's a long story."

Jack texted JB. *It's done.*

Hours later, NATO troops stormed the compound and unarmed the rest of Lofton's security forces. Thomas and the Brotherhood, including Kaiya, quietly slipped out of Spain and went back to the *Scorpion* with the help of Dawson and their new secret weapon. Kaiya never returned to JPL. The Brotherhood now had a new deadly enemy in Napoli Chenko.

Once safely on board the *Scorpion*, Erd hugged Thomas while no one was looking and whispered, "I'm pregnant."

www.ingramcontent.com/pod-product-compliance
Lightning Source LLC
Chambersburg PA
CBHW020606180626
46810CB00007B/2672